HUNT monsters DO magic AND FALL IN love

a contemporary fantasy triptych

A.M. WEALD

ISBNs: 978-2-9594881-08 (paperback), 978-2-9594881-15 (ebook).

Cover design, editing, and formatting by A.M. Weald
amweald.com

Character art by Nastia // NeedlesslyCryptic
instagram.com/_.anastasia.e._

Proofreading by Brittany Bookworm Editing
instagram.com/brittany_bookworm

Fonts used in the text of this work include *Yrsa*, *Rosarivo*, and *Sarina*, licensed under the OFL. Cover and titling designed in Canva under their Content License Agreement.

A shorter version of "The Hunter & Her Girlfriend" was originally published by Cinnabar Moth Publishing in the anthology *A Cold Christmas and the Darkest of Winters* under the title "I just want to spend Christmas with my girlfriend" and is available in print, digital, and audio format.

Date de la première impression : octobre 2024
Dépôt legal 1er publication : octobre 2024

This one's for me.

Author Note

The content of these stories may be emotionally challenging for some readers. Should you need them, a list of content warnings can be found on the next page.

I wrote the original version of "The Hunter & Her Girlfriend" after a year of being unable to write due to depression and medical brain fog. The idea came to me from a prompt of sorts, a contest on the private critique website Scribophile that asked writers to blend two different genres in unexpected ways.

I don't celebrate Christmas or generally consume Christmas-themed media, but I was partly inspired by the Hulu movie *Happiest Season*. The genres I meshed were fantasy and thriller, but there is also adventure, sapphic romance, family holiday, and mythology/lore mixed in. This story ended up placing third (out of 22) in the contest. This was therefore not only the first thing I'd written in a year, it was also my first writing that ever placed in a contest.

Years later, I wanted to expand upon this silly little story. And thus, the other two stories included in this collection were born.

The stories in this triptych are meant to be fun, but are not exactly cozy. They're cozy-adjacent, with some raw emotions mixed in.

Content Warnings

Alcohol use, drug use mention, cigarettes

Adult language and situations

Fire

Scars

Electrocution/shocking

Folklore-based monsters

Demons and ghosts

Teen pregnancy

Child abandonment/adoption

Secrets within a relationship

Domestic abuse mention

Murder in self-defense

Character injury and death

HUNT monsters DO magic AND FALL IN love

a contemporary fantasy triptych

A.M. WEALD

Father Winter is a malevolent ancient spirit. The veil between worlds really is thinnest on Halloween. Dragons exist, but they're just demons. And demigods walk the earth, protecting humanity from it all.

The Hunter & Her Girlfriend

2020. When Margot invited her new girlfriend Emili to meet her parents over Christmas, she should have realized that Father Winter might show up... and try to kill her.

The Maiden & The Liar

1990. When a hunter fails to slay Father Winter, Poe's family holiday road trip is waylaid by the ensuing dangerous blizzard, and they're forced to take shelter in a highway rest stop. Thank goodness other teens are there, including a cute boy and his high school hockey team.

The Healer & The Hammer

1989. Nora's on the run for murder, hiding out at a hunter academy where famous Thom "The Hammer" is currently contracted to hunt and kill the Jersey Devil. A rare healer, she's assigned to his detail because the guy is a f*ckin' demon magnet. Great.

Hunt Monsters, Do Magic, and Fall in Love *is a collection of modern fantasy stories interrelated by family—stories with myths and demons and ghosts (oh my), and with romance and secrets and lies (and someone dies).*

the Hunter
& *her* Girlfriend

Sweater Weather

2020

IN HER BEDROOM illuminated by the grey winter morning, Margot glowered at the fuzzy cartoon yeti on her ugly Christmas sweater.

"We meet again..." she grumbled at the snarling beast.

It wasn't the yeti's big teeth, sharp claws, and curled horns that made her cringe. The yeti was cute! It was the bright red knit and flouncing silver tinsel tufts that caused in her a visceral repulsion whenever she looked at the garment. But the sweater was a gift from her parents (mostly a gag gift, as they adored ugly Christmas sweaters and had a few themselves) and it had won her second place at a Christmas party a few years back.

Margot laid the sweater on the bed then peered at the open bedroom door, listening.

Emili was still downstairs, readying the house for their vacation. Unplugging the TV and computer, unplugging all the kitchen appliances save for the fridge, and even setting up timers so that lamps in the bedroom and kitchen turned on and off at specific times. All the mundane worries that Margot had never thought of until now.

As Emili busied herself downstairs, Margot closed the bedroom door.

It was now or never.

Inside the closet, curtained by dresses she never wore, was an old book bag. Inside, stashed at the bottom beneath random old textbooks no one would ever look for, was her dagger.

Aside from the dagger's silvered steel blade, the weapon itself was nothing special. Not a priceless heirloom, and certainly not ancient. But Margot's grandmother had gifted it to her on her seventeenth birthday, had it specially commissioned to mimic the shape and weight of the blade Margot most admired in her grandmother's own collection.

'*To the beginning of something new, and terrible, and wonderful,*' her grandmother had said to Margot upon gifting the dagger.

How right she had been.

Though Margot had seen her fair share of skirmishes, she had yet to experience genuine danger, the kind her parents and grandparents and family friends whispered and warned about.

Every winter since her seventeenth birthday, Margot prepared for the biggest battle she could ever face. And every winter, she asked herself why she didn't just move to Costa Rica, or Fiji, or the wilds of the Amazon. Anywhere that it didn't snow.

Like her mother always said: *Danger was everywhere.* But winter? Winter brought out the worst the otherworld had to offer.

Despite the danger, Margot remained in New Jersey. She couldn't leave her family anyway—couldn't abandon her inherited duty. Plus, it would have been too difficult to give up soft pretzels and pork rolls.

While using her body to block the line of sight from the bedroom doorway, she removed the dagger's leather sheath to inspect the weapon. The handle was a smooth, unadorned ebony, and fit perfectly in her grip. It wasn't by any means a substantial weapon, but would be better than nothing in an emergency. Other, larger weapons were stashed elsewhere in her home, under floorboards and within false walls in various closets and cabinets.

The chisel-ground edge had been sharpened last spring. She typically trained and fought with swords, but daggers were more convenient for a road trip, and her parents had their own arsenal.

Margot wrapped the sheathed dagger in her Christmas sweater and zipped up her suitcase. Eyes closed, she took a deep breath, trying to shed the guilt that weighed upon her conscience.

Trying. Failing.

The bedroom door opened and Margot jumped, her black curls bouncing around her face when she looked across the room.

"You ready?" Emili asked.

She was wearing one of those cute Scandinavian sweaters, a line of patterned green moose stretching across her ample chest. It looked old, but it was much more festive than Margot's plain black shirt.

"Yeah," Margot said, smiling at her adorable girlfriend of eight whole months—a new record. "I think so."

Emili wrapped her plush, wool-covered arms around Margot's more angular body and gave her a warm kiss on her cheek. "C'mon. I can't wait to meet your folks."

Sip n' Split

THE DRIVE FROM Trenton to Buena took an hour on a good day, and Margot knew the way by heart. But Emili, being from Oregon, had never seen the New Jersey Pinelands. And because she loved slower, scenic routes, she requested they drive south through the state forest rather than take the faster major highways that passed through populated areas.

The Pine Barrens, especially in the winter, weren't much to look at. The US 206 was a typical, narrow state highway sparsely populated by houses, farms, gas stations, and frozen marshland. Under the blanket of snow lay sandy soil, and for much of the way, the road was flanked by mixed forest, not just evergreens.

Margot hadn't mentioned it to Emili, but rural highways like the 206 also meant varied threats, least among them deer.

Oh, if only it were that simple...

On the outskirts of the township of Tabernacle, with only a half an hour to go until their destination, Margot's bladder said *absolutely not* to waiting, so she pulled into the Sip n' Split parking lot.

"I'll be quick," she said, unbuckling.

"Well *I'm* going to get myself a terrible truck-stop coffee," Emili announced.

"Your funeral."

Emili shot finger guns with an exaggerated wink.

Emili bounced on her toes, attempting to warm herself as she waited in line at the outdoor coffee stand. Her black leather jacket was usually fine for warmth when worn over a sweater, but today the wind was unforgiving and blew her light-brown hair in and out of her frozen face.

"Run Rudolph Run" played on the radio behind the counter. Emili actually hated this song—most Christmas songs, in fact—but the tune was so ingrained in her brain that she didn't even realize she was humming along until it was her turn to order.

No, Emili didn't care about Christmas or Hanukkah or any other holiday, save for New Year's Eve and Halloween because they were fun. But she did enjoy the idea of a holiday centered around being with family, which was exactly how Margot and her family celebrated Christmas— areligiously.

As Emili paid for her drink and waited for it to brew, a snowflake twinkled down. Another. More. She squinted up at clear, bright blue from behind her sunglasses. Odd that the other patrons in line didn't seem to notice or care that flurries were falling from a cloudless sky.

Peppermint mocha in hand, she made her way to the car. A gust of wind slapped at her black leather jacket, and ahead of her, a tiny snow twister swirled between two parking lines. As she walked past it, a tendril of snowflakes seemed to reach out to her, and an icy wisp grazed her neck and tugged her hair.

Then came the whisper on the wind: "*Emmmiiillliii...*"

Her grip on the coffee cup faltered and it fell, the contents splatting across the asphalt. She ran the rest of the way to the car, slammed the door closed, and quickly buckled her belt.

"I thought you wanted coffee," Margot said.

"I…" Emili locked her gaze onto the dashboard, onto the void behind a slatted air vent. "Changed my mind. I don't think I should have any."

"Ooookay…" Margot started the car.

As Christmas music jingled from the car's satellite radio, Emili said with a laugh, "I think I'm nervous. I was hearing things, seeing things at the rest stop."

"Seeing things?"

Emili waved it off. "It's just nerves."

Margot smiled. "You don't need to worry. My parents will love you."

As Margot pulled onto the highway, "Let It Snow" transitioned to "The Chanukah Song."

"Why aren't there more Hanukkah songs?" Emili asked. "I actually do like Adam Sandler's song, but can't there just be more?"

"What would you want them to be about?"

"Anything but dreidels? I don't know. I just feel outnumbered. And why are they even playing it? Hanukkah was weeks ago."

"Smells like pandering."

Emili lightly booped Margot's nose, and then they sang along to the live recording, each of them having long since memorized the lyrics of the annually overplayed song.

As the song transitioned to "Feliz Navidad," the sky clouded over, and it began to snow.

"Again?" Emili took off her sunglasses. "It's supposed to be sunny all week."

A chill ran through Margot.

"It flurried at the rest stop," Emili said. "Was weird. No clouds. And I saw a snow devil."

"Snow devil!?" Margot hadn't meant for the question to come out a shriek, but, really, how else was she supposed to react?

"You know, like a dust devil. But with snowflakes."

Emili's explanation did nothing to calm Margot's nerves.

The blizzard quickly worsened, and the highway's sudden whiteout demanded Margot's attention. She turned on her fog lights but, failing to see where she was driving, decided to pull over.

"What the hell?" Emili said, looking at her phone. "There's nothing on the radar. Not one cloud."

In front of the car, a shadowy figure emerged, cloaked in swirling snow. The shadow crept closer, and the steering wheel squeaked under Margot's grip.

"Emili," she said, "I need to tell you—"

"What is that?" Emili sat forward, peering beyond the windshield.

Margot eyed Emili. "You can see it?"

The shadow, a condensed swirl of snowflakes, grew brighter by the second.

"It's the snow devil again," Emili said.

So...this was it. The moment Margot had been warned about. The moment she had prepared for since she came of age nearly a decade ago. And she had never warned Emili.

She should have come clean that time when she came

home with a nasty scratch instead of claiming it was an unfortunate run-in with an exposed screw.

She should have come clean that time when Emili found a '*super fancy*' dagger in her desk and used it as a letter opener.

...She should have never started dating Emili in the first place.

Margot swallowed the guilt that had formed a lump in her throat, then whispered, "That isn't snow."

Emili trembled as she pressed her fingers to her neck, to the place the tendril of snow had touched.

In front of the car, a girl appeared: young, expressionless, silvery and luminous, dressed in white furs from head to toe. The blizzard swarmed around her, seemingly obedient.

Margot unbuckled her seatbelt and popped open the back seat access to the trunk.

"What are you doing?" Emili asked.

Margot didn't answer her as she rummaged around her suitcase and pulled out what looked like a knife.

Emili lurched away. "The hell!?"

"Whatever happens," Margot said, holding her gaze, "don't leave this car. If I don't come back, drive to my parents. Their address is in the GPS. If the GPS signal is lost, if the car dies, *stay in the car*. It's protected. My parents will find you."

"What are you talking about? Protected? What's going on!?"

"Don't leave this car! Promise me!"

"Okay!"

Snowflakes swirled into the car when Margot opened the door. The black tresses of her hair whipped about in the wind, framing her soft, fearful smile. "I love you."

Emili yelled for Margot and tried to grab her, but the seat belt brought her to an abrupt halt as the car door slammed closed. She unbuckled then watched, heart pounding, as Margot disappeared into the blizzard.

Her fingernails dug into the car seat as she leaned forward, watching, waiting.

Two minutes. Five.

Margot hadn't told her how long to wait.

Nine. Ten.

Mariah Carey's "All I Want for Christmas Is You" played yet again. Emili watched for movement, any movement outside the car, but there was nothing but blizzard. Just as she thought to climb over to the driver's seat, the snow stopped, and the clouds dissipated. The sky was blue and bright again as if nothing had happened. Other travelers had also pulled over during the squall and were now continuing on their way. Emili scanned the snow-blanketed stretch of highway ahead, but Margot was nowhere in sight.

The driver's side door opened.

Emili screamed.

"Wow," Margot said as she slumped onto the seat.

"Where the hell...? You scared me!"

"Sorry." She put her sheathed knife in a center console cupholder, then caressed Emili's cheek with icy fingers. "Are you alright?"

Emili nodded despite her trembling.

"Okay." Margot started the car. "Let's talk." She pulled onto the highway. "I'm sorry that I waited to tell you. I didn't think I would have to so soon. It isn't something we just tell someone. But with everything that's happened..."

The snow devil. The whisper. The girl.

"I wasn't just seeing things at the rest stop, was I," Emili said.

"I... I'm not sure. I thought only people like me and my family... What did you see just now?"

"A blizzard. And a pale girl." Emili looked at Margot. "Why was there a girl?"

Margot tapped on the steering wheel. "It wasn't a girl. Not anymore. She's a spirit. We call her the Snow Maiden. Russians call her Snegurochka." Margot glanced at her weapon. "The dagger is silvered steel. Scares away spirits, or can kill them if they take corporeal form. I ran her off, but she'll be back. I only pissed her off."

"A spirit," Emili whispered as she watched the roadside trees flick by. "Are there others like her? Other spirits? Other...things?"

"Yeah," Margot answered gently. "There are others."

Of all the angels and demons and spirits and saints, it *had* to be the Snow Maiden, a day earlier than expected. And wherever the Snow Maiden appeared...

Margot dreaded what came next.

Emili had fallen silent. The annoyingly perky "Jingle Bell Rock" blared over the radio, and Margot angrily turned it off. She wanted to reach for Emili's hand, to attempt to comfort her, but thought better of it.

Another mile stretched by until Emili spoke. "So...what are you, exactly? Some kind of superhero?"

Margot cracked a small smile. "Kind of. But not like in comics or anything. We're human. But some of us are stronger than others, and others can manipulate the elements. Create blizzards, rain, fire. My mom can heal wounds. I guess you could call it magic. People like my mom, they've been called witches, but we call them elementalists. Mom's an earth elementalist. Me, I'm not all that powerful. Can't use magic or anything, but I can fight. And my dad, he's *really* strong. People like me, my parents, and my birth parents, we're hunters. That's the collective term for people like me and my family—hunters." Margot glanced at Emili. "You know all those times I went to judo?"

"You were actually fighting demons in an alley?"

Margot almost laughed. "I was training. It just wasn't judo. Self-defense classes, mainly, and weapons training. Taught by another hunter."

"How many people like you are there?"

"A bunch. There are academies and everything. And outside of the academy system, we find each other through networking. Easier now with the internet, my parents tell me."

Emili fell silent again, and Margot considered her words carefully. "I'm sorry I kept this from you. I should've told you about my family, prepared you for this. Our first winter together, I knew this could happen. And now it's fucking happening."

"What? *What* is happening?"

Margot let out a great sigh, and with it most of her nerves. "Every year, wherever temperatures get to freezing, me and my family and others like us, we have to be prepared. The Snow Maiden is just the harbinger: her arrival means Father Winter is coming."

Emili's face scrunched. "Father Winter. Like…Santa?"

"No. *Not* like Santa—I'd love it if that's all we were dealing with. Some people think he and Father Winter are the same, but they're not. All those old white men of myth got lumped together over time as stories were passed on, and the idea of Father Winter merged with Santa Claus."

Margot shifted in her seat. "Father Winter, Jack Frost, Jokul, Ded Moroz… If anyone ever fails to ward him off when he arrives on the winter solstice, that area of the world gets devastated by winter storms. Buildings destroyed. Plants and livestock killed. But beat Father Winter in battle and he goes away until the next winter solstice. We can never know where he'll show up again." Margot peeked at the rear-view mirror. "I guess this year it's our turn."

"Is he a spirit, like the girl?"

"He's more like a god, old as winter itself."

Silence filled the car until Emili asked, "Are these things hunting you?"

Margot gave a stiff nod. "Yeah. Kind of. It's like they can sense us. That's the main difference between hunters and humans—hunters can see spirits and demons, while humans can't. My parents raised me to be ready. For Father Winter, and for others like him."

"And you're going to have to fight him."

Margot nodded again, then asked, "Will you call my parents for me?"

She unlocked her phone and handed it to Emili, who stared at it before scrolling through the contact list. Margot could hear the phone ringing, and with a quick glance, she caught Emili's thin frown and sad, worried gaze.

"Hi, sweetie!" Margot's mother Nora chirped over the speaker. "Everything alright? Lunch is just about—"

"Mom!" Margot shouted. "Mom. They're here. They found me."

Home for the Holidays

EMILI DIDN'T KNOW what to make of all that she was learning about Margot and her family, but during the rest of the car ride, she had built a picture in her mind of a fancy, Bruce Wayne–esque palatial estate, gated and buttled and overwhelming. But Margot's parents' home was as mundane as houses could get: a modest two-story rural colonial with white siding and a detached garage in the middle of a modest rural neighborhood. White string lights outlined the borders of the house and swirled around a lone evergreen on the front lawn.

Upon opening the front door, Thom, Margot's father— white-haired, average in stature, and wearing an Aran sweater that showed off his familiarity with weightlifting— smiled at Margot and Emili in turn. He pushed his tortoiseshell glasses up his nose, grinned proudly, and in a sarcastic, dry and jaded tone, said, "So, I hear something *wicked* this way comes."

"Oh, ignore him." Nora brushed a hand down her long, wavy brown hair that draped over the shoulders of her turquoise blouse. "Come in, come in." She hurriedly waved Margot and Emili inside.

Despite Margot's protests, Nora took her daughter in her arms and squeezed tightly and at length before pulling back to cradle her face between her palms. Her smile was equal parts sad and proud. "I hoped this day would never come for you, but you've trained for this."

Thom sandwiched Emili's offered hand between his in not so much a shake as a consolation. "You've had quite the introduction to our family. Come on, we'll have a nice chat about it over coffee. You're gonna need it."

The entranceway sparkled with holiday decor—tinsel, garlands, string lights, and candy canes. The aroma of mulled wine filled the house, and Emili wondered if she could get drunk instead of caffeinated.

Thom led them into the kitchen, where a large, dark-red candle burned unassumingly on the corner counter: the disappointing source of the mulled wine aroma.

"Are you trained in combat, Emili?" Thom asked in earnest.

"Um." She looked nervously at Margot. "No?" Her answer had come out sounding like a question, because normally people didn't ask strangers if they were trained in combat.

This was all getting ridiculous.

"There's still time to get some lessons in." Nora smiled at her warmly, her gaze lingering. "I'm sorry we had to meet under these circumstances. But, given the circumstances, I'm so glad you're here, with us."

Margot pulled her mother into the living room as Thom explained to Emili the difference between mythology and reality when it came to the Snow Maiden and Father Winter.

Quietly, Margot said, "I think Emili saw her—the Snow Maiden."

"Uh-huh." Nora nodded slowly, her face long with

concern. "Okay. Interesting. And why do you think that?"

"We were at a rest stop, and she said she was hearing and seeing things—a snow devil, like a dust devil, but the sky was clear blue. Then, on the highway, she definitely saw the Snow Maiden. I thought regular people couldn't see her, just the snow she brings."

Nora pursed her lips. "People can't see spirits and such, usually, unless they're hunters. Or, if they do, they forget immediately after."

"But…" Margot started, unable to finish the thought.

Emili, like Margot, was twenty-six. If she was a hunter or elementalist or anything in between, she would have known by now. She would have been hunted by those that often hunted Margot and her family.

Right?

"Coffee's hot!" Thom shouted from the kitchen.

"So," Thom said to Emili. "Margot's briefed you on our, uh…" He smirked. "Responsibilities?"

Sitting at the broad mahogany dining table, Emili frowned into her hazelnut drip coffee and said, "Kill Father Winter, save the town?"

"Yeah, basically." Thom sipped his black coffee. "When spirits and demons take corporeal form, they're vulnerable, but can do a real number on us, too. Injuring them just pisses them off. You gotta finish the job—'kill' them. Though sometimes killing them just means they can't leave the otherworld again for a while. For seasonal spirits, that period of rest is one year." He chuckled. "Sometimes two years, if you give them a good trouncing." He winked at

Nora, who stuck her tongue out at him then grinned. "Unfortunately, like most gods and personifications, Father Winter can't be permanently killed."

"Hunters have been keeping tabs on them for centuries," Nora said. "Where they are in the world. First, we communicated with letters. Then phone calls. Now we have an encrypted group chat, and many attend the annual summer meeting, one held on each side of the equator."

"They always show up where hunters live," Thom continued, "certainly on purpose. They can't stay away—something in their *raison d'être*. The winter spirits almost always haunt the northern hemisphere, but they've popped up in Australia and New Zealand, sometimes Argentina, South Africa. Even once in Antarctica. Wrecked that research station. Slaughtered penguins."

"Big furry asshole," Nora grumbled.

Thom snort-laughed.

"Why?" Emili asked, and everyone stared at her. "Why do they attack at all? I can understand that they're pulled to you, have a drive to fight you, but why do they devastate a land with winter storms? Why are they destructive? There must be a reason. Do they hate humanity or something? Hate animals?"

Thom grimaced. "It's not that simple. Think of Ol' Jack Frost as a necessary evil. Sure, if he kills whoever he's targeted, blizzards and ice devastate the land. A punishment for weakness, perhaps. But if he's defeated, he grants that area a gentle accumulation of snow. Either way, wherever he goes, he ensures a flowery spring and a fruitful harvest months down the line. He just makes you earn it, basically. Though now that I say this out loud, it doesn't really explain why he went to Antarctica." Thom shrugged. "Got bored, I guess. Immortality must be rough. Can't even appease him with trinkets and cookies and virgin brides anymore. Now, he's out for blood."

"I'm sorry," Emili said, "did you say 'virgin brides'?"

Thom nodded. "That I did, my dear Emili. Most of them froze to death, of course. The dark and twisted history of humanity."

Emili downed her coffee, and really wished for some of that nonexistent wine.

"The important thing to know," Nora said, "is what Father Winter and the Snow Maiden are capable of. Frostbite, blizzards—"

"Hail," Margot added. "Ice daggers."

"Ice daggers," Emili repeated.

"Daggers of ice," Thom confirmed. "Oh, and spears, too. Or javelins, I guess. Anything that can be thrust or thrown and used for piercing. Think sharp icicles of varying length."

"Don't forget ice shards," Nora said.

"Ice shards!" Thom pointed at Nora excitedly. "I forgot about the blizzard of ice shards."

"It's what took out the penguins."

"How...!?" Emili shouted, and everyone waited for her to finish her question. "How can you fight something like that? How can you defend yourself against *ice shards*? Do you wear armor? Margot had a *dagger*." She gestured at her girlfriend. "How can *a dagger* help?"

"Well, it's better than nothing." Thom turned to Margot and added, "I'm glad you thought of taking one with you."

Margot gave her father a small smile. To Emili, she said, "Shields help, if you can wield one. But, no, we don't wear armor. And apparently the ice shard blizzard was a one-time thing. I wouldn't worry about that."

"Why would I worry about that?" Emili asked. "These things aren't after me."

As soon as she said it, she remembered the tendril of snowflakes and the wind whispering her name.

Nora, in all seriousness, said, "They might be. And if they are..."

"Best to be prepared," Thom finished.

The room fell quiet, and a chill shot up Emili's spine.

With a gentle slap of his palms on the dining table, Thom stood. "Weapons. Let's show Emili the armory."

"Silvered iron or steel weapons," Margot explained, "is the only way to battle a spirit and win. Or magic, of course, particularly water or fire, but me and Dad aren't elementalists."

Thom opened one of the locked cabinets in his office to unveil an arsenal of modern and medieval weaponry. Emili gasped and backed away from the double-bladed great-axe, the scimitar, the javelins. Thom set out several weapons on a tall, central wooden table, its surface scuffed and scratched.

"I've used one of those before," Emili said, pointing at a crossbow. "My brother has one to hunt deer."

"Oh?" Thom placed a case of bolts on the table next to the crossbow. "Then I guess we know what your weapon will be. We'd better start training—the solstice is tomorrow. In the morning, we'll head out to the forest to cut down a Christmas tree. We always do that on the day of the solstice." Thom stuck his hands in his pockets and chuckled. "If Li'l Sweetie or Ol' Jack do pop up, at least it'll be away from the 'burbs. Somewhere they'll do less damage."

"You've fought him before?" Emili asked.

"Nora has. And she's got a gnarly scar on her back as a souvenir."

Nora rolled her eyes, and Emili noticed a faint, linear scar crossing one side of her neck.

Emili frowned, then turned her gaze back to the weapons.

"I'd feel better if you came with us tomorrow," Margot said to her, "but you can't just stay in the car. The Snow Maiden is one thing, but the car won't help you if Father Winter targets you."

"Think *Jurassic Park*," Thom said, "only it's a giant furry god incarnate."

"I'd definitely feel better if Emili came with us," Nora said. "And I think she would feel better with a weapon in her hand."

"I have the feeling Emili will manage just fine," Thom said.

A warmth washed over Emili as fear, anger, and love rose within her in equal measure. She approached the table and picked up the crossbow, learning the weight of it.

"Okay," she said. Turning to Margot, she added, "I'll join you."

Furious

MARGOT SAT ON the foot of her bed, watching Emili comb her hair in front of the small, antique maple vanity.

Emili had grown quiet after practicing with the crossbow, remained quiet during dinner, and even while watching a stupid Christmas movie.

The silent treatment gnawed at Margot's throat.

"Are you mad?" she asked, hoping to get her talking. "I would understand if you were pissed."

Emili paused her combing, then put her comb back inside her toiletry bag. She turned around on the little bench, her lips pressed together in deliberation. After walking the few paces to the bed, she sat beside Margot and clutched her hand, weaving their fingers together.

"Honestly?" Emili started, "I'm just scared that we might have to fight these things if they come for us, and there's really nothing I can do to help. I'm okay with the crossbow, but..."

"You're really good with the crossbow."

"With stationary targets."

They lay down in bed facing one another, hands clasped. The warm glow of the ceramic light-up Christmas tree on the night table behind Emili haloed her hair.

"I feel better knowing you'll be with us," Margot said. "Maybe it's just peace of mind, but... I don't know. You make me feel safe."

Emili nestled in close, burying her face in Margot's curls. "I feel safe with you, too."

Margot wrapped her arms around Emili, and her warmth chased away the chill left in her bones from earlier in the evening. "So, you're not mad?" she asked.

"Oh, I am," Emili said before kissing Margot's neck. "Furious." She kissed her earlobe. "Wrathful, even."

Margot laughed, shrugging away from the tickling sensation of Emili's breath in her ear. "It's okay to be angry. I would be. Just don't point that crossbow at me."

Emili chuckled, then kissed the tip of Margot's nose.

"So, tell me," Margot asked, curious. "Have you ever seen anything like the Snow Maiden before?"

"Definitely not."

"What about, like, shadows at the corner of your vision? Felt the presence of ghosts? Strange voices or odd, out-of-place weather?"

Emili shook her head. "No. I never even believed in anything like that until..." She paused and looked at the curtained window. "Well, until a little girl blizzard spirit stared at me from outside a car." She leaned in to kiss Margot's lips, then whispered, "I really thought I'd lost you in that blizzard."

Margot brushed Emili's hair out of her face and tucked it behind her ear. "There's a very real chance the blizzard will come for me again."

"Or me. They could be coming for me."

Margot pulled Emili close again, hugging her tight. "They'd have to get through me and my family first."

Fireball!

THE SKY WAS a bright blue with barely a wisp of cloud, and the orange hunting vests that Thom made everyone wear glowed. Even with all that sun and no wind at all, the day of the winter solstice was bitterly cold. Emili was thankful for her insulated boots as they crunched across the ankle-deep snow of the Pineland forest in search of the perfect Christmas tree.

Joining Emili, Margot, Nora, and Thom was a friend of the family, Kizzy, and Kizzy's partner, Lex, who happened to be Margot's self-defense and weapons training instructor.

'*Just in case,*' Nora had said.

'*The more the...less likely to die,*' Thom had added unhelpfully.

Kizzy, an air elementalist, was petite and strongly built, with greying dark hair shaved very short. Both Kizzy and Lex, who in contrast had a shock of fuchsia hair, were dressed for combat or camping or both in their thick vests and military-style trousers and boots.

Thom hummed a pleasant tune as he led the way through snow-weighted pines and naked oaks. They wouldn't venture far, Nora had promised Emili, not more than a mile from where Thom had parked his SUV at a roadside pull-off.

Thom carried a hunting rifle just in case a bobcat got a

bit too eager. Lex carried a shotgun loaded with silvered shot. Emili carried the crossbow on her back by a thick strap that crossed her chest, with a quiver of silvered bolts at her hip. Large, bladed weapons were illegal in the state, Thom had explained, after an incident some years ago involving a halberd and someone who was very much not a demon. But no one would question a hunting rifle and a crossbow. Their silvered daggers were concealed.

The New Jersey Pinelands, Emili had learned from Margot as they walked, stretched across the southeastern part of the state for more than 1,400 square miles, and only a small portion of that was inhabited. The rest was trees and sandy soil and grasslands and swamps. Anything from coyotes to beavers could be found in these woods.

Emili was anxious, and who wouldn't be, knowing that Father Winter might—and probably would—come for them. Well, not for her. Those spirits had no reason to target her. She wasn't a hunter or a witch or anything of the sort. This Snow Maiden, the spirit that supposedly called to her, tugged her hair, stared at her, was obviously mistaken. But, as Margot had said, they were vengeful spirits, and Margot had pissed off the Snow Maiden.

Marching into a forest alongside superhumans while carrying a crossbow just in case they were attacked by an old god was *not* how Emili had expected to spend her vacation. But she loved Margot—she'd *kill* for Margot, if it came to that. Knowing that Margot would do the same for her only strengthened her resolve.

"Not many dryads this year," Nora remarked.

"Nope," Thom agreed, and curled his arm around Nora's waist. "C'mon, Sparks. Let's find a good one."

Emili looked at Margot and mouthed, "Dryad?"

Margot grinned. "Tree spirits. The last thing you want is to take home a tree with a sleeping nymph in it. Dad sings the song, and they wake up and leave the tree. Then we put an offering by the stump in exchange for, well, taking that nymph's home. It's only fair."

Something darted across their path. Emili halted and clung to Margot, then glimpsed the tail end of a deer before it disappeared behind bushes. Thom and Nora had stopped, too, but then chuckled and carried on.

Emili followed them, but Margot pulled on her hand.

"You saw her?" Margot asked, her eyes wide

"Here we are!" Thom called from ahead, standing before a fir tree of about eight feet tall. He hummed his pleasant if a bit eerie tune, and the delicate crunch of galloping footsteps on snow faded into the distance.

Another deer, or so it had looked out of the corner of her eye. Was that a dryad? Did dryads look like deer? Emili was too overwhelmed and confused and wary to ask.

Thom had no trouble downing the tree with a saw, nor any trouble dragging it by himself all the way back to the road. As they finished fastening it to the roof of the SUV, it began to snow. A gentle, cloudless snow.

Everyone went silent and still, and the only sound was the thudding of Emili's hammering heart. She nearly gave in to the urge to hide in that SUV protected against malevolent spirits with the same silver-plated steel used in their weaponry. But Margot reached for her hand and squeezed it, offering her courage.

Gooseflesh prickled up Emili's arms when Thom said, "They're coming."

Quietly, calmly, Thom opened the trunk of the SUV and slid out a massive war hammer.

Nora, her expression stone-cold, pulled a longsword from the back of the SUV.

Margot chose a smaller sword, then pulled a dagger from her boot.

Kizzy carried a sword nearly as tall as they were, while Lex wielded two small battle axes.

Emili, terrified but ready—maybe—swallowed hard, then loaded the crossbow.

Flurries multiplied rapidly, and a blustering wind bowed the trees that flanked the road. A wisp of snow swooshed past Emili, then lashed like a whip at Thom's cheek. He cried out, pressed his gloved hand to his face, then slammed the trunk closed. An angry red gash, frostbitten at the center, marred his face.

"Come on out, kiddo!" Thom shouted at the sky. "And bring that old bastard with you!"

The wind carried delighted giggles, and a swirl of snow condensed to take the form of the Snow Maiden, silver and glowing. Clouds quickly covered the sky, and the driving snow evolved into a violent, blinding blizzard.

Kizzy, hand raised and palm pressing outward, seemed to force some of the biting winds away from the group and back at the Snow Maiden. This must have annoyed the spirit girl, as she shot Kizzy a stern glare then dissipated into snowflakes.

From within the forest, deep thuds sounded every few seconds, followed by the *crack!* of breaking wood. Louder, louder, like thunder from the earth, sending vibrations straight up Emili's spine.

Boom!

Margot's focus held fast to the grinning Snow Maiden while Thom and Nora faced the woods.

Boom!

Emili watched Margot for a clue, but knew deep down exactly what—who—it was.

Boom!

The pulsing thunder crescendoed and treetops swayed and snapped, then through the blizzard's veil emerged a growling giant with white fur, curled horns, and massive claws. As the yeti-like beast neared, it roared, sending a blast of ice that stung Emili's cheeks.

The Snow Maiden giggled. Emili whipped around to find herself only an arm's length away from the grinning, glittering spirit who, in a lilting voice, teased, "Grandpapa's here."

With startling ferocity, the Snow Maiden flung icicles at Margot and Emili. They ducked, but one pierced Emili's leather jacket into her shoulder, and she yelped from the sharp, burning pain. Margot lunged at the spirit girl, who again giggled and disappeared in a burst of snow. The icicle embedded in Emili melted, leaving a small, frostbitten wound and a hole in her jacket and sweater.

The Snow Maiden reappeared a short distance away, and Margot and Lex ran after her. In the other direction, Father Winter swung at Nora and Thom and Kizzy with a hand the size of their torsos and claws the length of their heads, but they dodged the attack, each taking a swing at his legs. The beast roared again and slashed at them in slow but powerful swipes.

Emili waited for a clear shot of Father Winter's face, aimed, then watched crestfallen as the crossbow bolt shot into the deep snow. She cursed, then reloaded. The second shot went wide. Margot and the Snow Maiden fought behind Emili as she took aim again. When she pulled the trigger, the weapon encrusted with ice, jamming, and the mechanism snapped.

Emili threw the crossbow to the ground. "Goddammit!"

Thom and Nora ran further up the road.

"I just..."

Father Winter stomped after them.

"...want..."

The beast roared, and the air shook.

"...to spend..."

The Snow Maiden giggled.

"...Christmas..."

Emili turned to the Snow Maiden.

"...with..."

Her fingertips tingled.

"...my..."

Flames ignited in her palms.

"...girlfriend!"

The Snow Maiden's eyes widened as two fireballs shot out from Emili's hands, whizzing past Margot and hitting the Snow Maiden in the chest. The girl's scream was cut short when she poofed into a gentle cloud of steam that rose to the sky.

Emili stared at her palms, then caught surprised looks from everyone. They all gawked at her, and she watched, helpless, as Father Winter landed an open-handed blow against Thom. The force sent him flying, and his body slammed into the side of the SUV. Nora screamed and ran after him, and Margot and Lex and Kizzy all charged the beast.

Emili's hands were hot. She again looked at her unburnt gloves, then removed one to find her palm completely fine, pale flesh entirely intact.

Margot's shouts pulled her attention back to the fight.

Father Winter had conjured an ice javelin. As he drew back, aiming at Emili, Margot plunged her sword deep into Father Winter's belly. The beast howled, faltered, then keeled forward. And with one ferocious swing, Kizzy opened the beast's neck.

The air crackled, and Margot turned to Emili, eyes wide, shouting, "DUCK!"

Margot curled into herself and Emili did the same, tucking her head as a blast of ice shards shot over her, nicking clothing and flesh. When the frozen stings stopped, when a nearby bird chirped, Emili looked up.

The blizzard had cleared. The winter spirits had vanished. The snowy road glowed beneath the noon sun, highlighting small patches of bright human blood.

Kizzy ran over to kneel at Thom's side as Nora pressed her palm to his chest, sending out a golden healing glow.

"I'm fine, darling," he insisted, though his grimace said otherwise.

Margot ran to Emili and grasped one of her hands. She examined it as Emili had, then squeezed it tight as Lex walked toward them.

"Are you injured?" Margot asked Emili, her own face bleeding from slivers of wounds.

Emili nodded to her shoulder, then looked at her hands again. "What happened? Did I...make fire?"

"I don't know." Margot pulled Emili close, and Emili buried her face in the crook of Margot's neck. "I don't know, but we'll figure it out."

"A friggin' fire elementalist?" Lex muttered to themself, still gawking at Emili.

Nora healed everyone's wounds, then took Emili in for a

long, tight embrace.

"I knew it," Nora whispered. "Thom sensed it the moment you met, and I just knew." She pulled back, still gently grasping Emili's shoulders. With the broadest grin, Nora said, "Welcome to the family."

Goddess

MARGOT WATCHED EMILI as she slept beside the comfort of the house's crackling fireplace, wrapped in faux fur blankets, hair tousled and wet from her long, hot shower. She had been so quiet on the short drive home, and it was no wonder—fighting an ancient winter spirit was not exactly what Emili had signed up for when she had matched with Margot on that dating app. But now, Margot couldn't help but wonder if it had been more than attraction and interest that had brought them together.

Emili had seen the Snow Maiden. Seen the dryads. Margot should have realized Emili was a hunter before the fight. If only she had known sooner, months ago. She wouldn't have had to keep her real identity a secret. They could have trained this whole time! But until the road trip, there had been no clues, not a single one.

Unlike Margot, Emili didn't know her birth parents. They could be anywhere, or nowhere. They could be anyone. Perhaps they had been young. Perhaps they had been terrified. Perhaps they died.

Were they elementalists, too? Had they met through secret social networks? Had they faced demons and spirits and monsters and ghosts? Had one of them been able to manipulate the elements like Emili had? This trait was inherited, a recessive gene. Neither of Margot's birth parents were elementalists, something she was actually grateful for—the skill seemed a lot of work to control.

What hit hardest about all these realizations was that Emili would never be able to tell her adoptive parents what had happened today, what she discovered today.

Margot pondered these things instead of sleeping, comforted by the soft sounds of Emili's fitless slumber.

Emili had fought the Snow Maiden and *won*. She had *created* fire. *Fire!* As if the universe decided there was an imbalance between the elements and, in their moment of need, bestowed Emili with the ability to manipulate the one element best suited for slaying winter spirits.

Margot didn't know anyone else who could create and manipulate fire. Only energy or earth, like Nora, and wind and water. Manipulating water was useful when fighting winter spirits—shattering their ice spears or turning the frozen weapons against the spirits. But fire...

Emili was special.

Emili was dangerous.

A shiver ran up Margot's spine, but not because she feared her girlfriend. No. She was afraid of how much the winter spirits would fear Emili, and worried that she would remain their target for as long as she lived.

Margot leaned in close to the sleeping Emili and lightly brushed her nose against her forehead.

"I love you," she whispered. "And I will always protect you, my fire goddess."

Friends in Warm Places

BEER AND FRIENDS, Margot thought. That was what Emili needed to help her absorb her new reality. Be surrounded by others who understood. Share a platter of nachos, and get very, very drunk.

Emili had met Margot's Trenton friends on several occasions, but only one of those friends was a hunter, and none of them were elementalists. Here in her hometown of Buena, and neighboring areas as well, hunters that were Margot's and Emili's age were plentiful, particularly because they were home for the holiday season, and Buena was a hunter academy town.

The group of young hunters found sanctuary in this sports bar, loud and bustling as it was. No one paid them any attention. No one could hear them talk.

"So let me see if I got this straight," Margot's childhood friend Teddy said. "Not only did you not know you were a hunter—"

"That's what she said, Teddy," Teddy's sister Lyra reminded him.

"—but you discovered you were a hunter while battling the fucking Snow Maiden?"

Emili shrugged. "I wasn't exactly handed a manual by my birth parents."

Margot laughed, but Emili's remark gave her an idea.

Teddy shook his head and sipped his beer. "Badass."

"Elementalists are the best friends to have," Lyra said. "*Especially* earth elementalists, and not only because they can heal paper cuts." She winked at Emili. "*So* many benefits to energy manipulation."

"I don't...don't understand?" Emili looked at Margot, whose ears and cheeks were burning furiously.

"Sparkle, sparkle!" Teddy said, flourishing his fingers at his boyfriend, Yanic.

Yanic winked at Teddy. "Aaanyway, Emili, if you're not meditating or doing *something* to release stress, you're going to want to start. I don't want to know how many times I accidentally started a rainstorm or blizzard because I was fucking pissed off."

"You're always pissed off," Lyra said.

With an air of false frustration, Yanic said, "I guess I need more stress relief."

Teddy rolled his eyes.

"Sparkle sparkle?" Emili asked Margot.

"I'll tell you later," she promised with a peck on Emili's cheek.

"Better yet," Teddy said, "have Margot's parents explain it."

Margot shot to attention. "Teddy!"

Lyra's face reddened with restrained laughter, and with Margot giving Teddy a kick on the shins and Yanic corralling him with a kiss, the subject was dropped, much to Margot's relief.

The absolute last thing she wanted to speculate upon was her parents' *sex life*.

"Yanic is right, though," Margot said to Emili, squeezing her hand. "With all that's happened, with all that might happen in the future—and wondering about your past—it's a lot to take on, a lot to unpack. It's okay to feel whatever you're feeling, vent that frustration or fear or anger. We're all here for you."

"I'm not really that angry," Emili said, and the hunters sitting around the table gave her skeptical stares. "I'm not," she insisted. "I suppose I should be. Angry with my birth parents. Angry at Father Winter. But I'm just not. I'm..." She smiled warmly at Margot. "I'm happy. Happier than I've ever been. Maybe it's the rush, or maybe it's Margot."

"It's definitely me," Margot said with a coy shrug, garnering laughter from the group and an elbow in the ribs from Emili.

When the laughter died down, Emili's smile faded. "I am scared, though," she said, and the group's mood shifted. "And a part of that fear does make me a little angry. But only because there's a chance those monsters could come for my family"—she turned to Margot again—"my new family, and hurt them, take them from me." Emili's jaw clenched as her lips set into a tight frown. In a shaking voice, she said to Margot, "I love you so much."

Margot reached for Emili's hand, squeezed it tight, and leaned in to kiss the love of her life.

"Well," Teddy said. "Shit."

"I'll drink to that," Yanic said.

Lyra whooped loudly, and Margot's friends clinked their pints in cheers.

Emili watched in awe as Margot threw one bullseye after another at one of the bar's many dart boards.

"How are you so good at this?" Emili asked her. "And *drunk*, too?"

Margot stared at her blankly when she said, simply, "Throwing daggers. They're actually my specialty, but don't work as well with winter spirits that can just poof into a swirl of snowflakes. It's hard to hit a moving target, even harder to hit vapor."

Margot barely had to size up her shot before making her throws. Emili's darts, which she lobbed at the board next to Margot's, were all over the place, most of them embedded in the pocked wooden wall.

"Back in college," Margot said, "I hustled this guy who was being an absolute *dick*, not even trying to whisper his racist, homophobic mouth turds. Got two hundred dollars off him in a double-or-nothing dart match. I would have preferred to slaughter him in an alley, but darts are less messy."

"Yes," Emili said, laughing, "because *mess* is the most concerning part of that little anecdote."

Margot cocked a brow at Emili, and without looking, threw a dart at her board, hitting the green circle around the bullseye.

"Would you?" Margot asked. "If you could. Well, you could. You can." She mimicked a fireball with her fingers and said, "Fwoosh!"

"Would I get messy in an alley, you mean?"

"Yeah." Margot collected their darts.

Emili's next dart arched nicely but inevitably pierced a black triangle—eight points, if they had been keeping score. She tried another dart. If she got a point for every time she hit the wooden wall, she would have a lot of points. Should she even be doing this after four—or was it five—beers?

Would she immolate a bigot in an alley? *Could* she, if given the chance?

The little hairs on the back of her neck bristled at the thought. "Let's not test my convictions before I fully understand what I'm capable of. I'd rather not be responsible for arson. This is a nice bar."

Margot grinned at her. "Fair."

That time, Margot got a bullseye without even a glance.

"*Convictions*," Teddy repeated with a devilish lilt. "Sorry, Em. Couldn't help but overhear."

"I was just telling Emili about that guy I hustled at darts back in college."

"Oh, that fucker." Lyra switched places with Margot and tried her hand at darts. "I wanted so badly to grab my sword from my car. *But*," she said with a sigh, landing a dart within the outer ring, "explaining to the police why a guy is run through with a broadsword isn't exactly easy." Eyeing Emili, she added, "*Trust* me, I've been there. Though in my defense, that guy made demons look *good*."

"We try to limit our defenses to daggers when out and about," Yanic explained. He leaned against a wide wooden post next to Teddy, spectating. "Too many people with mobile phones, you know?"

"Thankfully," Teddy said, "to most people, we just look like LARPers."

Lyra threw several almost-bullseyes.

"And regular humans can't see the monsters?" Emili asked. "What if someone records you fighting a demon?"

"To hear my mom tell it," Margot said, "most of the time, only hunters can see otherworldly beings. But if a non-hunter does see one, or witnesses a fight, the second they turn away from it or turn off that video they watched, they forget about it. If it's in writing, the non-hunter will assume it's bullshit, or fiction. It's a sort of…biocultural evolutionary trait, an otherworldly protection."

"Mystical gaslighting," Yanic said.

Margot nodded. "But sometimes people don't know they're hunters, and they see everything. Those people are the ones non-hunters think of as crazy. Thankfully, a lot of the time, other hunters find them and help them understand."

"So if demons and things go after hunters," Emili said, "why didn't they come for me? I was adopted by regular humans. I would have been an easy target."

"The more time you spend with hunters," Yanic said, "the more hunter you become, if that makes sense."

Lyra landed a bullseye. "It's why we come of age, so to speak, only at age seventeen."

"Except for the select few," Margot said. "My dad said demons started coming for him even as a baby."

Emili nodded, ruminating on everything she had learned over the last few days. "So. Spirits, demons, ghosts…" Her dart actually got close to the center that time. "Are gods real? Any of them?"

"They sure are," Teddy said. "Loads of them, all overlapping in myths as cultures evolved."

"But they fucked off outta here millennia ago," Lyra said. "Probably got bored."

"Things might make more sense," Yanic said, "if you think of hunters as remnants of the gods. A mortal, human link to the otherworld."

"And what else is real?" Emili turned to Margot. "Angels? Vampires? Zombies? Aliens?" She crooked her lips. "Werewolves?"

There was a lull in the conversation until Lyra laughed.

"Come on," she said. "Zombies? Zombies aren't real."

"Unless you count corporate drones," Yanic said.

"They're a metaphor for slavery," Teddy said.

"I want to believe aliens are real," Yanic said, "but the logic just isn't there."

Lyra slinked toward Emili. "What would you do if you learned that I was a werewolf?" She smirked and cocked a brow, then let out a low, almost-menacing growl.

"She's fucking with you," Teddy said. "We've never met a werewolf. Or a vampire."

"But they are real, sort of," Margot said. "Shapeshifters and sanguivores. Angels are just spirits, and not always benevolent. Most bits of folklore carry some truth to them."

A tingle of worry ran through Emili, but it faded when Margot grasped her hand. To the group, she said, "I think I need a stronger drink."

"That's the *spirit*," Lyra said with a wink.

Yanic winced. "Oof! Too soon."

Margot laughed and led Emili to the bar. "Come on, they make a mean mulled wine cocktail."

Emili groaned with preemptive relief. "Oh, thank *goodness*."

Pamphlets

LATE ON CHRISTMAS Eve, Emili sat by the fire with Margot, who presented her with a leather pouch. Emili opened it to find a dagger similar to Margot's, its blade gleaming against the firelight. She carefully examined the weapon, held its polished wooden handle, learned its balance, then looked at Margot, uncertain.

"Dad and I are going to train you to use it," Margot said. "And eventually swords, or axes maybe, as big as you can handle, if you want to. And Mom can help you with your magic. There are academies where hunters go instead of a regular university, but you don't *have* to go to one. Like, you can be a hunter or an elementalist and go to a regular university, be freelance... But if you do want to investigate academies, there's one not far from here. Oh—" Margot pulled from the case a small stack of pamphlets. "I asked my parents if we had anything. These were written by people like us. Guidebooks on how to use magic, how to fight. And updated versions of the ancient ones passed down. Our print shop guy is a hunter, too."

Emili bit her lower lip as she looked over the dozens of pamphlets.

The Ins and Outs of Throwing Daggers.

How to Overcome Your Fear of Fire as a Fire Elementalist.

How to Care for Your Silver-plated Weapons.

"Wow," Emili said, "there really is a manual."

"And there would be a lot more at an academy. An entire library of the stuff."

She set the pamphlets down and looked at Margot, whose face was alight with hope. But all Emili could feel was a renewed sense of dread. For herself, for Margot, for the world.

"They're going to come for me next winter," Emili said, "aren't they."

Margot took Emili's hand and traced the lines of her palm with a fingertip. "Maybe. They're vengeful spirits. But if Father Winter returns, we'll be ready."

Emili looked again at the dagger, at the pamphlets.

Your Magic and You: What Your Element Says about Your Inner Self.

Emili almost laughed, and her worry bloomed into ardent resolve. With a flutter of her fingers, a gentle flame danced within her palm. She glanced up at Margot, and with a determined smile, nodded. "When Father Winter returns, I'll be ready."

Welcome to the Family

ON CHRISTMAS MORNING, Emili unwrapped her gift from Thom and Nora: an ugly Christmas sweater, all bright greens and reds and shining gold, with a cartoon snowman winking, unafraid of the snowflakes falling around him.

the Maiden & *the* Liar

The Blizzard

1990

THE BLIZZARD WAS still howling and battering the car when Poe's parents returned, shoulders hunched, faces long and paler than usual, and swords hanging low at their sides. Before they opened the hatchback, they spoke to one another in voices so hushed they were silent beyond the barrier of the closed car doors and windows. Bundled up in their high-winter gear, they looked like angry, colorful potatoes. Poe couldn't read lips, but she was certain they were talking about her, or talking about what to tell her…or not tell her.

Something bad had happened.

Poe only knew the basics: why Mom and Dad and all her grandparents had collections of bladed weapons that shimmered and sometimes tarnished, needing to be polished or replated. That all their weapons were silver-coated steel. That they were used to fighting things that went bump in the night and, sometimes, the day.

Her parents had been mostly candid with her from the age of ten, when she learned that Santa Claus was the spirit of an actual saint, and the Easter Bunny was an old European god who could shapeshift. So now, at the age of fifteen—just a year and a half shy of being inducted as a hunter—Poe deduced the reason her parents were disheartened.

Today was the Winter Solstice.

Father Winter had come and gone.

And a hunter was dead.

Poe and her family had been at a rest stop en route to Pop-Pop's house when the first snowflakes began to fall. No one but Poe and her parents had batted an eye. No one else could have known that snowfall on the solstice was the harbinger of chaos.

Because Poe had no weapon with her, she had to retreat to the protection of their little car, for it too was plated with silver, a literal shield against malevolent spirits.

Though her parents had searched for the spirit, armed with weapons that would surely raise alarm, they couldn't have found Father Winter, for they both still lived. If Father Winter had been slain, Poe knew, the blizzard would have receded. But the world beyond the car was veiled by white, and the wind howled. Somewhere not far, the winter spirits had targeted another hunter. And with that hunter's death, Oregon would be buried under snow.

After Poe's parents put their weapons in the back of the car and slid into their seats, her father started the car, and Christmas music recommenced mid-song from the FM radio. Her parents remained silent, and Poe sulked in the back seat, resenting the exclusion.

Poe's mother removed her red knit hat and tossed it onto the slant between the dashboard and windshield. "We can't keep driving," she said as she combed her fingers through her long, dark hair. "Just wait a little while. It will probably stop soon."

"Or it could last days," Poe's father replied through gritted teeth, pushing his gold-rimmed eyeglasses back up his nose. "Why didn't he come for us?"

"Maybe he was scared of you." Poe's mother was grinning, almost flirting, but that didn't calm her husband's sour mood.

"Well, now we've got this stuff to deal with."

"This is a rest stop," Poe's mother said. "With restaurants and toilets and dining booths. Let's just make ourselves at home until this blizzard blows over."

The rest stop had a donut shop, a McDonald's, a newsstand, and a row of vending machines. And throughout the building were clumps of helium-filled red, green, and white balloons along with cheesy Christmas decorations and one huge plastic menorah with seven plastic flames atop its nine plastic candles. A handful of families and a boy's high school hockey team had the same idea as Poe's parents—wait out the storm.

Day became night, and the shops offered a free meal and water to the stranded patrons, and coffee for the adults who wanted it. Poe's father used the payphone to call his mother, to no doubt explain to her what had happened. She could then activate her phone tree, alerting the network of hunters so someone, somewhere, would learn that someone they loved was dead.

"Hey," called a boy's voice from behind Poe.

She turned to see a tall and handsome but pale and lanky teenager, his brown hair several shades lighter and much shorter than her own.

"We're recruiting all the kids to see if they wanna hang out," he said. The boy looked at Poe's parents. "If that's alright."

Poe's father was still in a huff, so her mother said with a smile, "Yes, that's fine, if Poe wants. Just don't go outside."

The boy laughed. "We won't. Our coach is over there." He pointed to a stocky, bald man holding a lively discussion with another stocky, bald man. "If you wanted to talk about hockey or the Gulf War or something." He grinned at Poe. "So?"

Poe, bored out of her mind, eagerly said yes.

"I'm Emil," he said.

One evening turned into another, and another. Even ambulances and police cars were having trouble navigating the whiteout roads, getting into accidents themselves. The shopkeepers were stranded along with the patrons, but other than being annoyed, they did not fret. There was plenty of food and water, so long as the blizzard didn't continue for much longer.

Poe was grateful for the other kids and teens. If she had been the sole young person in that rest stop, she might have gone completely cocoa puffs.

Over the course of several exceptionally long days, Poe learned that Emil was kind, and sweet, and fun and funny, and that he was a really, really good kisser. He liked that she was plump in contrast to his leanness, and found it 'cool' that she lived here in Oregon—he was from California.

"I didn't think Californians would play hockey. Don't you all surf out there?" Poe laughed and, mimicking a surfer dude accent, said, "Right on, duuude."

Emil smirked as he leaned over her, and she lay back on

a flattened cardboard box on the janitor's closet floor—one of the few spaces they could be alone.

"Right on, dude," Emil murmured before kissing her.

Poe untied the leather cord from around her neck, then gave the necklace's single blue blown-glass bead one final look before looping the cord around Emil's wrist and tying it tight.

"To remember me by." She brought his wrist to her lips to give the blue bead a kiss.

Emil smiled, then leaned in to kiss her. "I don't need a bead to remember you by, but I will wear it until the day I can return it to you."

"And I'll hold you to that promise." She kissed him back. "I really like this bead."

When the blizzard finally died down and the roads were plowed and drivable, the boy and his cohort continued on their way.

He would miss the cute girl in torn jeans and a ragged Oregon State University sweatshirt. It had pained him that he had to lie to her and give her a false name, as instructed by his handler. That he couldn't tell her that he and the other boys were not hockey players but bound for a special academy, one he couldn't risk disclosing the location of.

He was sad, because he would likely never see the girl again. Even if he did, it would be better if he ended up with a hunter, like himself. It was dangerous to spend one's life with someone who couldn't properly defend themselves from spirits and demons and monsters that might do *him* harm. Spirits that, usually, only hunters could see.

And he was sad because one of his friends—a friend *his age*—had died in that battle against Father Winter, and while snowed in at that rest stop, he had to pretend nothing was amiss for the sake of their collective secret. Pretend he was down because they had lost a hockey match. Pretend that he hadn't almost died, too.

As David Bowie crooned from his Discman, and to pass the time until he and his cohort arrived in Alaska, the boy formed a tiny flame with the snap of his thumb and index finger, then scorched a message into the back of the vinyl-covered bus seat: *L+P*, with a heart surrounding them.

The Fire Station

1991

POE HUGGED HERSELF tightly, compressing the ache out of her breasts. She mustn't give in, no matter how much it hurt to turn her back on her daughter.

And so in the middle of the night, with the shrill cries of her newborn calling after her—begging, accusing, blaming—she walked away from her neighborhood fire station, convinced by her family that it was the right thing to do.

Until the firefighters found the infant, she would be fine, protected from the autumn thunderstorm by a cardboard box, swaddled snug and warm in Poe's green moose-parade sweater.

Tucked within the folds of the sweater was an apology, and the only other thing Poe and the father could give their child: a name.

The Academy

2003

THE NORTHERN CALIFORNIA Hunter Academy was to welcome a fire elementalist today into its scholarly ranks.

Poe didn't even believe they existed, having never met one herself. She had read about fire elementalists, but to her, those tales were barely more than fiction.

She would have to see it for herself, the supposed control, manipulation, and creation of fire this Liam person could do. But it would have to wait until after the welcome assembly, a pompous gesture that the principal handler would certainly never put on for any other type of hunter. Not even earth elementalists—healers—received such ceremony.

Poe expected that the new elementalist would perform a demonstration, as she couldn't possibly be the only skeptic. Even if she was, all elementalists loved to show off.

As she rounded the corner to her classroom, she slammed directly into a tall, lanky man with light brown hair. The exams she had been hugging to her chest fluttered across the entire hallway cross-section, but she left them where they lay.

Poe gawked at the man before her, so familiar and, yet...

Recognition hit him in the same moment it did her,

given the widening of his brown eyes.

"Poe," he breathed out, and his jaw remained dropped.

"Emil!?" The name, the question, the accusation came out a shriek.

The woman with him, the principal handler, smiled and said nervously, "Uh, Poe, this is Liam. Our newest Professor of the Elements. Fire! Can you imagine? We can make proper introductions later, but for now we're running late for a meeting."

The handler gave Poe a little wave as her heels clip-clapped down the hallway. The man Poe had known as a boy looked back at her as he departed, the fluorescent ceiling lights highlighting the lines and crevices etched in his face by regret and dismay.

Poe's gaze dropped to his right wrist. On it was tied a dark cord, and under the bright lights glowed a single blue bead.

the Healer & *the* Hammer

Sparks

1989

SHE REMAINED ATOP him, straddling his lean waist, her palms stuck to his cooked flesh. The stench of him and his pool of piss mixed with the sweetness of his melted polyester clothing and the singed nylon rug. A bouquet of death.

With a *squick*, her hands were free.

She was free.

And she was fucked.

The Healer &
The Hammer

NORA HELD A cigarette to her lips with one hand and a bag of frozen peas to her cheek with the other while her handler, Larry, made a call to a guy he knew, someone who could get her out of the very stinky mess she'd made. He asked a question into the phone's off-white plastic handset, then looked across his desk at her.

"Yeah. Alright, one sec." Leaning close to her, Larry asked quietly, "Is there a"—and he whispered—"body?"

Nora swallowed hard, then nodded.

"Blood?" he asked.

Nora's long brown hair swooshed over her nylon windbreaker as she shook her head.

Larry conversed on the phone long enough for the peas to soften and for her to notice that the wood paneling of his office was buckling in the middle.

"It's taken care of," he said, finally hanging up the phone. "Your boyfriend just bought a bus ticket to Vegas, leaving tonight. And since no ID is needed for said bus, no one will second guess our field agent of the same height, weight, and complexion traveling in Vern's stead, checking in to Vern's hotel, and enjoying the slots and free drinks for a nice, long vacation."

"A believable lie," Nora said with a laugh, and winced. Talking hurt.

"So, how'd you do it? Without bloodshed, I mean."

Nora hadn't thought about it much, whether or not to tell Larry or anyone else fully what had happened. The less everyone knew the better, as far as she could figure. In truth she barely understood it herself, how a man as big as Vern could be brought down by her, so small in comparison.

She looked at Larry, at his dark sprigs of hair set in a combover atop a sunburnt scalp that fluttered in the soft breeze of the small oscillating desk fan every few seconds, and managed a small, ignorant smile. "How'd I do what, Lar?"

His robust form jostled in laughter. "Right, right. Okay, listen. I need you to get outta here, too. Not right away or it'll look suspicious when Vern decides to stay in Vegas forever. But in a week or so. We can help you pack and move—no worries there. There's actually a couple academies that could use a healer such as yourself, if you don't mind going back to that grind. Do you have a preference between east coast or west?"

"No."

"Okay. I'll call Angie over in New Jersey. She's the handler I'm gonna hook you up with. There's some shit going down out thataway, and they don't have a healer anymore."

"Do I wanna know what happened to said healer?"

"Nah."

"'Kay."

"But they've got this hunter out there—you've heard of The Hammer?"

Nora laughed. Yeah, she'd heard of The Hammer, named

so because he'd commissioned the most impractical weapon—a giant silvered steel war hammer—and surprised everyone when he could actually wield it efficiently, and lethally. Though that wasn't the only reason they called him Hammer...

The guy's name was Thomas, and he'd shown up some years ago, supposedly an orphan out of Brooklyn. That in itself wasn't special—the children of hunters were so often orphaned. What was special about him was that he was exceptionally strong, was seven feet tall, had biceps as big as watermelons, and had stark-white hair despite being only a year older than Nora at twenty-nine.

She'd never seen a photo of the man. All of the rumors were probably bullshit.

"So, what exactly is going on out east?" she asked. "Not another apocalypse, I hope."

"Ha! No. Just some troubles down in the forests of south Jersey. Residents have been complaining, going missing; unexplained fires, deaths. I don't wanna say we're worried, because we're not, but we might start to worry if this keeps going, ya get me?"

"Sure, Lar."

The man's posture softened. "I'm gonna miss ya, kid."

Whenever Larry said *kid*, Nora melted a bit. Her real father would have never been so affectionate. Her real father was likely sipping Mai Tais on a Mexican beach, or something equally unhelpful.

"Gonna miss you too, old man," Nora said, maintaining that little bit of satirical distance she needed in order to not start sobbing.

Hunters like Nora and her mother, and her mother's mother and so on, were said to be earth elementalists. But unlike those who could manipulate fire, water, and air—shooting fireballs, summoning a raincloud, taming a cyclone—earth elementalists couldn't shoot rocks across the room or dig tunnels, though that would come in handy. No, what Nora and her maternal line could do was heal. And as Nora had most recently discovered, she could generate sparks of electricity.

Could her mother make sparks?

Did it get her killed?

Like most elementalists, Nora's training began before she could walk, and she'd graduated from a hunter academy by the age of twenty-two, no different than any other American rich enough to afford college. But no one had ever taught her about elementalists creating *electricity*. Was it just another form of earth energy manipulation? The fireball version of lighting a gentle campfire?

Other than energy manipulation, Nora had a combat medic's training: setting bone fractures and dislocated joints, suturing wounds, diagnosing and treating internal bleeding and concussions... With energy manipulation she could heal major wounds to an extent, stave off infection, but doing so took a lot out of her. Along with knowing how to defend herself with or without a sword, knowledge of basic emergency medicine was necessary for those times when that golden light of what she called magic just refused to glow. All hunters, no matter their natural-born skill, went through basic medical and weapons training.

Nora hadn't trained with any of these hunters at the New Jersey academy, didn't see any faces from her graduating cohort among the instructors, and obviously wouldn't know any of the students. Knowing someone other than her new handler Angie would have been nice. Knowing anyone in New Jersey would have been nice. But while some of her friends had been living along the east coast, she had no idea where they were these days. They rarely wrote letters, and long-distance phone calls weren't cheap.

It was unlikely anyone here knew who Nora was, *what* she was. Nobody wore badges or name tags or color-coded uniforms; everyone just wore whatever they wanted. To all the others here, she was just a newly arrived hunter, of which there were several.

So Nora quietly ate her dinner in the mess hall of this spartan boarding house in the middle-of-nowhere New Jersey with her back to the wall, listening to conversations but otherwise keeping to herself, occasionally scanning the room for a familiar face and eyeing the many silver-plated steel weapons that lined the lower walls, some of them tarnished.

The swords and axes and crossbows were mostly there as decoration, but also as silver wards and, in a pinch, resources. But academies were rarely attacked. All those hunters in a single place? Even inexperienced inductees were capable of taking down a demon.

The sound of the tortilla chips crunching inside her mouth drowned out much of the hall's din, but when the room fell deathly quiet, the crunch gained the attention of the others at her table, who shot her nervous and disapproving looks.

"What?" she said softly, mouth full, chips still crunching.

Nora followed the room's collective gaze to the mess hall's double-door entrance where several people had entered. Last among them was a man of average height with shoulder-length blond hair tied back low, a build much stronger and light skin more tan than Nora's, wearing thick black-rimmed glasses and a Eurythmics band t-shirt. They all received a portion of the day's soup, a scoop of peas, slices of bread, and a slab of pot roast, then sat at the only empty table.

"I had heard he was here," one of the hunters at Nora's table said, "but thought it was just a rumor."

"Hellooo *daddy*," another hunter said, and many at the table laughed.

"Hammer me baaabyyy," someone whisper-sang.

Unless The Hammer had superhuman hearing, he remained blessedly ignorant of what was being whispered about him across the mess hall from what must have been the handler's table, judging by Angie sitting there, cozying up to the young man who seemed to just want to eat.

Nora was hypnotized by Angie's thick form and bulging biceps as she attempted a haphazard preen of her mussy strawberry blonde braid. The handler caught her gaze, paused, then motioned for her to come sit at the handler's table. Angie had to repeat the gesture for Nora to confirm that she was being summoned.

Ignoring the murmurings of her tablemates, Nora walked her meal tray to the front of the hall, dumped her trash, then warily approached the handler's table.

"Nora," Angie said sweetly, the scent of her imbibed wine wafting. "Sit! Meet Thom."

Thom, she'd said, as if she was old chums with the guy. Did The Hammer prefer Thomas? Did he expect Nora to address him by his cult-hero epithet? Could she dare call him *Thom*?

Nora turned to The Hammer, smirked, then said dryly,

"Hey, Hammer."

The young man with nerdy glasses, grey-green eyes, and a strong, scruffy chin looked at her, unreadable. But then his tight lips quirked up, and he flashed her a delighted grin.

Matching her tone, he said in a voice not nearly as deep as she'd expected, "Hey, Healer." Squinting at her face—the bruised half, with a black eye that Vern used to joke brought out the blue in her eyes—Thom added, "*Niiice* shiner."

So this was The Hammer.

How anticlimactic.

Over dessert and wine, Thom, as he preferred to be called, spoke on the topic of spirits and demons and such like he'd memorized an encyclopedia, and maybe he had. All these academies had libraries full of lore and hunter knowledge. Nora hadn't visited one since she graduated. Didn't see the point.

Danger was everywhere. Everyone was dangerous.

What else was there to know?

Thom had been contracted a few months ago to take care of trouble in the forests that surrounded the academy, an area called the Pinelands. Apparently he was good at diagnosing and disposing of otherworldly problems.

Tomorrow, Nora would tag along with Thom, Angie, and two elementalists deep into the Pinelands to follow up on a recon unit that had been sent out a couple days ago to track a suspected demon. But tonight, she wanted nothing more than to forget.

Shame all she had was a pack of smokes.

After dinner, she sat on a wooden outdoor dining table, feet on the bench, silvered dagger in her boot. She lit her cigarette with a lighter she'd found abandoned in a parking lot, then basked in the wafting smoke.

From his second-floor private apartment, Thom watched Nora where she lay on the table by the big oak, smoking. It was late, and they had an early morning ahead of them. He considered going out there, reminding her that she had a responsibility to the other hunters. But he wasn't her boss. He wasn't anything. Who was he to explain to her how to do her job?

It was impossible not to worry about her, though, considering why she was here in the first place.

A knock sounded at his door.

"Yeah," he said.

In entered Kizzy, a petite air elementalist who had put their coarse black hair in two low, thick braids, their preferred combat hairstyle.

"Hey," they said. "You ready for tomorrow?"

Thom stood from the little bench at his window. "Yep," he said lazily while stretching. "Were you briefed on the details?"

"Yeah, I'm good." Kizzy closed the door behind them. "You need a release? 'Cause I'm *tiiight*." They clenched their fists in front of their chest, then dragged a palm across Thom's abdomen.

Thom grasped their hand and held the palm flat against him. "It's late, Kiz," he said through a sigh, "but if you can be quick—"

"If *I* can be quick?" They laughed. "That all depends on you, *Hammer*."

He rolled his eyes, then tripped forward as Kizzy yanked him by the shirt toward his bed.

After Kizzy left, fully unclenched, Thom went to pull the

window shades but saw that Nora was still outside, stargazing perhaps, drawing constellations above her face, pointing out the stars to herself.

The lit end of a new cigarette brightened briefly as she inhaled. Her breath billowed, a dragon lacking fire.

The Jersey Devil?

"THAT'S WHAT THEY were tracking?" Nora said, her voice bouncing along with the armored truck as it rolled down the bumpy, sandy road. "The Jersey Devil?"

"The one and only," Thom said. "Or...one of many. No one's entirely sure yet what we're dealing with. Hard to know sometimes until you kill it. But if it's ol' J.D., it's just the one demon."

"Dragon," Kizzy said. "It's totally a dragon. What else could be burning down those cabins without getting caught?"

"Arsonists in the middle of the night," Thom snarked.

"It's definitely The Jersey Devil," Angie hollered to the back of the truck from the driver's seat. "But that doesn't mean it isn't also a dragon, or something like a dragon."

"It could be Mesingw," Talia said. "The masked spirit of Lenapé lore. I was reading about him."

"He wouldn't be setting houses on fire," Kizzy said.

Talia eyed Kizzy calmly. "He might, if people have been disrespecting the forest."

"We aren't fighting anything today, not if we can help it," Angie said, "but we need to be prepared for anything, which is why I brought the brains—me, the brawn—also me, and maybe Thom—"

"Thanks, Ange."

"—the ice princess over there—"

Talia furrowed her brow. "Hey…"

"—and the hurricane." The handler nodded at Kizzy.

"Sounds like we're putting together a band," Thom said.

Nora rolled her eyes.

"Lead guitar, clearly The Hurricane," Angie said.

"Ice Princess, gotta be keyboards," Thom said.

"I'm a *water elementalist*," Talia insisted.

"And The Hammer on druuums!" Kizzy roared, punching Thom in the shoulder.

Thom laughed, then narrowed his eyes at Nora in contemplation.

"Don't look at *me*," Nora said. "I can't carry a tune."

Angie laughed. "Alright, al—"

The brakes shrieked as Angie slammed the truck to a halt. Thom fell onto the floor, Nora fell onto Thom, and Kizzy and Talia both fell onto Nora.

"Fuuuck," Kizzy moaned. "Angie, what the hell?"

Angie didn't answer. When Nora climbed back onto her seat, she realized why Angie had braked so hard. Standing in the middle of the road, shimmering in the sunlight of the bright autumn morning, was a perfectly white stag.

"That thing just saved our lives," Kizzy whispered.

The stag eyed the truck, then looked down the road the other way, took one step toward the side of the road, then vanished as if it were made of nothing more than clouds.

Nora knew that spirit animals were an actual thing, but damn.

"What do you mean, Kizzy?" she asked. "It saved us from what?"

Kizzy pressed their lips into a tight line, then said, "I guess we should find out."

Everyone exited the truck, bearing their weapons of choice. The final door slammed shut. Then in the distance, someone screamed.

Thom had sensed it the second Angie slammed the breaks.

Demon.

A scream followed by a high-pitched roar from the forest confirmed it was near. Very near. As Thom reached behind his back for his hammer, he heard a forceful *whoosh, whoosh, whoosh* before a winged form briefly shielded the sun as it flew overhead.

Nora stood next to him, and he instinctively reached for her. He wasn't going to let that thing take this healer, too.

"Is it coming back?" Kizzy asked.

It...wasn't.

The itch, that prickle of pain that always plagued Thom whenever a demon or spirit drew near had since faded. Why had it fled? Usually demons were overly eager to fight him.

"I don't think so," Thom said. "But I'll let you know if anything changes."

The *smell*. Bacon and burnt hair and gasoline.

Nora smelled the bodies before she saw them, and she might have keeled over were it not for Thom's grip on her upper arm.

"It's—" Nora didn't want to say it. "It's burnt people, isn't it."

Thom sighed, and let go of her. "Yeah, I think it is." He gave her and Kizzy an empathetic glance. "Come on, Healer.

Someone might still need you. Though…" He looked around. "I kinda doubt it."

"Barry!?" Talia screamed as she ran further up the road toward a dark mass of something—someones?—that would have created an impasse for the vehicle, or at least would have forced Angie to drive over the mass.

Nora flinched at the crunch of bones and squish of guts sounding in her mind.

"Barry's her boyfriend," Kizzy explained without any hint of emotion.

Bodies. So many bodies. Barry was gone, no longer a person but a crisped husk of one. So was that person, and them, and them… Beneath the bodies, what had been sandy soil had melted and cooled into a gruesome, blood-tinged sandpapery glass. Up ahead alongside the road were the melted remnants of a Humvee turned on its side.

Were these the hunters of the recon unit, come here to find this devil? Was Nora about to face an actual fire-breathing dragon?

"Kizzy," Nora said. "That deer, you said it saved us. You think it was telling us to turn back?"

"That's what it does," they said. "Gets in your way for a reason."

"So we're in the right place, then."

"Or the worst place. Same thing for us, I guess."

Talia was sobbing at the side of one of the bodies. How she'd recognized that ex-person from yards away Nora had no idea.

"It's them," Angie said. "I checked a dog tag. Recon 151. All of them. Shit."

Nora clutched her new dog tag under her shirt.

"Don't worry, Healer," Thom said, his smile almost

smug, or trying to look smug. "I doubt our luck is bad enough for *two* troops to be incinerated the same day on the same spot."

"You're not helping," Kizzy said to him. "Come on, lets"—they coughed and swallowed hard, their olive complexion suddenly grey. "Shit, the smell. I can't."

"Sit it out, Kiz. Keep watch and tend to Talia." He turned to Nora. "You okay with the smell? We should get these people off the road until they can be collected."

The smell. No, she wasn't okay with it. But for reasons she wasn't about to explain to The Hammer, she also wasn't incapacitated by it.

"Come on," she said to him. "You get the shoulders, I'll get the feet."

He wrapped a black Tears for Fears bandana around his lower face. "There's disposable gloves in the truck."

As they dragged a body to the side of the road, she caught Thom's gaze that lingered uncomfortably on her and not, as it should have been, on the roadside foliage, or the charred body, or the sky. His mouth was covered by that bandana, but she would have bet her dinner he was smirking.

When they laid the body down, she said, "Nora."

"Hm?"

"My *name* is Nora."

"Yes, I know." His cocked brow hinted at annoyance.

"Not Healer," she continued, "not Nora the Healer, just Nora. And definitely not Elianora. Only my grandparents get to call me that."

Thom said nothing as they carried another fragrant body. Nora very much wished for a bandana of her own.

"Elianora," Thom said. "It's pretty."

"I said *not*—"

"Why not Ellie? Or...Lia."

She had to pause, laying the body down halfway to the roadside with a huff.

"So," Thom continued, "Lady Elianora the Healer..."

"Yeah okay. Keep it up! See what happens."

He grunted as they picked up the body again. "Where are you from?"

"Are you seriously"—she huffed again—"trying to hold a conversation with me right now?"

"Only seems fair—everyone knows my business. It also preoccupies the mind."

The third body was smaller. Nora didn't want to think about why, didn't want to know these ex-people.

"I'm from the Midwest," she said, "and now I'm here."

"Well, then. Lovely to make your acquaintance, Lady Elianora, Healer of the Midwest and more recently of New Jersey."

"Alright, Hammer, you asked for it."

"That's the spirit."

"What's so special about you that you get assigned a healer?"

"I get contracted to a lot of dangerous cases that usually end up with someone getting hurt."

The fourth body was the heaviest yet, but Thom didn't seem to notice.

"Is that what happened to the previous healer?" Nora asked. "They got hurt?"

He didn't answer her, and when they set down the body, Nora huffed and puffed and stretched her muscles. Thom just stood there, like an asshole.

As they grappled with the final body, Thom said, "Yeah,"

his voice unusually soft. "She got hurt."

Those four words were the first genuine emotion Nora had received from The Hammer. But she didn't like how deep his gaze ventured, and left his side to check on Talia.

Tea

NORA COULDN'T SHOWER enough, couldn't scour enough.

The *smell.*

The stench of charred human flesh and hair had sunk into her very soul and would not wash out. But the water ran cold, so she rinsed and towel dried, then wrapped her towel around her, tucking it in between her breasts.

The bathroom was large and industrial, or military more like, and all-gender inclusive. Nothing new—it was the same at her academy. In these bathrooms everyone walked around half-naked, or sometimes whole-naked, and Nora had long since gotten used to seeing bodies and body parts of all sorts and sizes.

After brushing her teeth, she sent herself to bed, a glorified cot in the academy's hostel where she couldn't sleep.

The *smell* was in her brain, a punishment, and all she could think about was not the bodies but Vern, screaming as she laid her hands upon his chest and crotch, shocking the worst bits of him to a crisp long before his heart gave out. Vern, caught dick in hand, giving himself to others, giving Nora's money to others. *Vern,* slugging her in the face for the last damn time when she told him she was leaving. *VERN,* when it hurt so much but he didn't stop...

Nora didn't know this building well, nor the grounds it

was part of. But she slipped on her shoes, and in her night clothes she ran from the hostel, outside into the rain, needing to wash the smell off, wash *him* off, shed herself of the life that was, that should have never been.

She'd let it happen. Let *him* happen.

Never again.

Her palms tingled, then burned, then crackled, and with a great release, ten slender bolts of electricity surged from her fingertips, scorching the ground.

Lightning erupting from hands was definitely not what Thom expected to see when he went outside to check on Nora.

He had heard rumors of elementalists who could both create and manipulate lightning. Mainly these talents were limited to erotic fiction written by hunters such as Kizzy who only wished they could manipulate energy in such a way. But it made sense for a healer to create sparks. Healing magic, as Thom thought of it, was nothing more than urging the energy of a living thing to repair itself. And living things were nothing more than elements and electricity.

Nora stood with her back to the building, arms out to her sides, letting the rain wash over her. He could barely make out her lean form against the blackness of the grounds beyond.

"Impressive," he called out from the front stoop. Nora whipped around, her chest heaving with rapid breaths. "They know you can do that?"

When her breathing slowed, she answered, "No."

In the distance, lightning crawled across the clouds.

"Come on," he said, and the answering thunder rumbled. "I'll make us some tea."

Nora sank into the warmth of the mug between her palms and gorged on the little spiced cookies that Thom had pulled out from behind the Tupperware. For a long while, Thom didn't say anything. No questions about the lightning she'd made, no lecture about wasting her healing energy.

With his tortoiseshell glasses folded on the table, Thom drank his tea and ate his cookies while relaxed against the metal folding chair.

"You don't have to go to the funeral tomorrow," he said, "if you don't feel up to it."

"It wouldn't be my first."

Thom eyed her, wholly unreadable as usual. "That's chamomile tea, by the way." He smiled at the mug, not at her. "Will hopefully help calm your nerves. How are they, by the way? Does it hurt? When you..." He smirked and flourished his fingers in waves in front of his face. "Make the sparks fly?"

She huffed a laugh. "It does. A little, at first. Like those pins and needles feelings. And then there's heat, and a fullness, and it punches away from me."

"Is it new? The lightning."

Nora caught herself before answering. "Very," was all she said. "Do you have anything like that? Something that makes you a little..."

"Different?"

"Dangerous." She pressed her lips together, deliberating how to approach the questions she had. "You're stronger than others. Is it for a reason? Do you, like, manipulate gravity or something? Too much testosterone? Born on Krypton? Do you 'Hulk out'?"

"Are you asking if I could hurt you?"

His eyes locked on to hers. That question, his directness and insight, caught her off guard. She didn't answer him, had to look away, at her mug.

"So," she said, avoiding his question, "you're just…kinda big and strong, and have good stamina? That's it?"

"You sound disappointed."

"Imagine finally meeting Hercules and he's just some guy."

Thom half-winced, half-grinned.

"Sorry," Nora said quickly. "That was mean. It's just— you don't exactly look like a half-dragon demigod."

He choked out a laugh. "Aren't we all *demigods*?" He said the word like he was mocking it.

True, some believed all hunters were demigods to a varying degree, depending how far removed from the divine source they were. No one really knew—everyone had their own version of the truth.

"Anyway," he continued, "dragons don't exist, so I can't be half-dragon."

"Then what did we see today if not a dragon?"

"Demon. They're always just demons."

Nora sat back in her chair, watching him. "Why were you awake?" she asked.

"Couldn't sleep."

"Worried about something?"

He smirked. "Always."

She tilted her head and couldn't shed the soft smile she knew she was giving him. "You wear that smirk like armor," she said, truly seeing him, understanding the man behind the living legend.

She had to smirk a lot, too.

Thom looked into his mug like he was disappointed at its emptiness. "I think we should try to get some sleep." He stood, and the chair lightly scraped against the tile. "I'll walk you back."

Wood

THE RECON TEAM, people Nora had never met, were given a collective funeral at the academy, though their bodies and belongings had all been returned to their families. Most people weren't wearing fancy black clothes. They just wore whatever, but kept it dark, out of respect.

Talia had disappeared during the night, her bedroom cleared out. It wasn't at all uncommon for hunters to leave— living out a quiet life in the suburbs making minimum wage at a Blockbusters didn't sound that bad compared to academy life.

Nora had only been in New Jersey for two nights and she was already submerged in the stench of death and swimming in a sea of grim, wary faces. And the devil-dragon-demon haunting the Pinelands was still out there, incinerating hunters and regular folk alike.

When someone began to sing some sappy song Nora's mother would have loved, Thom slipped out beyond the double doors of the gymnasium that doubled as a non-*demon*-ational chapel, as someone had graffitied over the real sign. Nora, being more hungry than heartbroken, followed.

Thom was out of sight by the time she reached the hallway, so she made her way to the kitchen. While she ate from that same secret stash of spiced cookies, she heard the slow procession of *whack grunt whack, grunt whack thud, whack thud thud.* With several more cookies wrapped in a paper napkin slipped into her jacket pocket, she followed the sounds outside, meandered her way around the academy's grounds, then spotted the source.

Thom. Shirtless. Chopping wood.

His back was to her, didn't notice her as he brought the woodcutting axe down onto an uncut log then tossed the cuts into a wheelbarrow. On a distant bench, Nora lit a cigarette and basked in the glow of the day's remaining warmth. By the time the cigarette burned down, she had been joined by others, all appreciating The Hammer as he chopped a winter's worth of wood.

"I'm gonna marry that man," someone said.

"I've already named our babies," said another.

And yet a third chimed, "Martillo. Spanish for Hammer. That's what I'd name our kid."

"Weirdo," someone else said.

Nora held back a smirk, snuffed out the cigarette on the metal bench, and left the group of people she didn't know to approach the person she did.

Thom had been ignoring the onlookers, just as he always did. They still hadn't gotten used to his existence, and that's all this was. Him, a person, existing, venting.

He knew it was Nora approaching by the smell of cigarettes and leather, and he found himself suddenly nervous. No one ever just...walked up to him, talked with him. No one except for Kizzy, who had called him out on all his shit from day one. Same with Nora. With everyone else, it was just staring and giggling, winking and blushing, "accidental" touching, and sometimes glowers or sneers. And it was starting to get old.

Nora stood before him, puffing her cigarette, her eyes doing the smirking that her preoccupied lips couldn't.

She blew the smoke out to her side then, dryly, said, "Hercules and one of his many labors." Then came the actual smirk he was waiting for.

He huffed a laugh, leaned the axe on the chopping stump, then retied his mussed hair. "Someone has to do it," he said, then set back to work.

"Need help?"

"The cuts go in the wheelbarrow."

And so she helped, singlehandedly, cut by cut, the other hand moving the cigarette to and from her lips.

"They always ogle you like that?" she asked.

"They're fairly common, the oglings, yes."

Her laugh was low and throaty, like her voice.

"You've got quite the fan base," she said. "I guarantee every single one of those people would lick the sweat off your torso right now, given the chance. Their comments are bordering on harassment."

"Oh, man." His ears and neck flushed hot. Was she *trying* to fluster him?

"They're also naming your babies," she said.

He froze mid-swing with the axe. "My *babies*?"

"Yeah, you know." She puffed one last puff then flicked the butt to the dirt and ground it out with her boot. "All those babies they're gonna give you. Or adopt with you." She turned to wave at the onlookers by the benches, who scattered the second Thom waved at them, too.

Nora laughed, and he laughed with her.

He neglected to mention that, thanks to his vasectomy a few years back, he would never have to worry about giving anyone babies.

Together they walked the short distance to the cut wood pile, him behind the wheelbarrow and Nora beside him, then added to the pile that was protected by a roofed storage shed.

Thom still hadn't decided what Nora's game was. She was, perhaps, the most veiled person he had ever met, aside from himself.

Like Kizzy, Nora obviously wasn't threatened or impressed by him. Just the opposite, it seemed. And as with Kizzy, he would gladly accept Nora's apparent offer of friendship, something he rarely found and was quite honestly desperate for.

There was just that pesky problem of him being instantly, frustratingly attracted to her.

And now, as she sucked on the side of her thumb after being jabbed by a splinter, as she let out a gentle whirl of golden light around the hand, all he could think about was her licking the sweat from his chest as her golden light wrapped around him.

But when the wood cuts were piled up and the wheelbarrow emptied, Nora gave him a casual *See ya later* muted by teeth that held a fresh cigarette in place.

Kizzy came to Thom that night as Kizzy often would. And, as Kizzy often would, they encouraged him to think about someone else, anyone else. Because this thing between them wasn't anything but lonely and embroiled bodies winding around each other, winding down.

These last two visits, he thought about Nora.

He shouldn't. For so many reasons, he shouldn't.

But how could he not?

"I think Nora digs you," Kizzy said, after, with their head in the crook of his neck.

"Spy," he said, and Kizzy laughed.

They leaned back and gazed across the bed at him with their big brown eyes that didn't belie their soft smile. "You should see that through. You never know. Just...watch yourself. Angie will have a cow if you can't concentrate on a mission just 'cause you're worried about your girlfriend."

And then Kizzy slipped away as they always would, never staying longer than physical needs demanded.

Just a Demon

ANGIE WASTED NO time in sending out several more teams to hunt and hopefully kill the Jersey Devil or dragon or whatever it was. They spread out to cover more ground, radios ready to call out scheduled checks. Thom and Nora were joined by three other hunters, while Kizzy and Angie led two other troops.

When they reached the stretch of road where they had retrieved the slaughtered recon unit, Thom shivered. But not from any sense of imminent demon. His reaction was from the physical memory of how much he had wanted to run from the scene, to drive all the way back to Brooklyn and take up cheesemongering.

But he had slapped on a smirk and the attitude that went with it, hoping that his air of bravado would help the others do what had to be done. It hadn't worked with Talia; her reaction was understandable. But it had with Nora and, eventually, with Kizzy. Angie...well, she didn't need any help in the bravery department.

This Jersey Devil character was no big deal, he had said. Definitely just a winged demon, he had said. And it was true, that last part. But a demon that could blitz an entire unit? He worried that this was one of those once-in-a-millennium happenings when an actual army would have to be mustered to battle a long-asleep foe. Thankfully, the creature was more likely to be a lesser demon than an old god.

He and others had scoured the library for any hint of what big bad would come out of hibernation or hiding once in a long while and crossmatched that with what big bad could set things aflame.

Demons, like some lesser spirits, were wicked, violent creatures. In their true, ethereal form, they were weak but largely invulnerable, only *annoyed* by silver, and 'killing' them only sent them back to the otherworld until they regained strength to return, if they so chose. But once demons became corporeal, taking on the form of just about anything they wanted, they were strong—sometimes *extraordinarily* strong—but vulnerable, risking becoming mortal.

The Jersey Devil was supposed to be nothing more than a colonial-age political scandal turned legend, but it became or perhaps had always been connected to indigenous lore. At this point, it was impossible to disentangle one from the other, and in the end *what* they were dealing with might not matter—everything otherworldly succumbed to silver, and everything could be weakened or injured with fire or ice.

Claims of sightings of the devil happened as recently as thirty years ago without any discernible pattern as far as timing. So if this was the Jersey Devil, the thing just came out and caused trouble whenever it wanted.

And that meant it was powerful.

And pissed off.

"You ever think we should wear armor?" Nora asked. "Or maybe soldier's uniforms."

"Uniforms attract too much attention," Vanessa said.

Paulo laughed. "And our huge weapons don't?"

Thom grinned back at Nora. "Flame-retardant clothing isn't good enough for ya?"

"Is it good enough to counter whatever melted that sand into glass?" Nora bit back.

They all looked like anachronistic barbarians, with their modified medievalish weaponry combined with flame-retardant blue shirts, black pants, and bright orange hunting vests.

"I dunno," Thom said. "Was the recon unit wearing flame-retardant clothing?"

"Nope," said the fifth hunter in the group, Heather, who carried a massive crossbow.

The plan was, if they found the devil, to lure it to the ground. Thom was apparently good at the luring part—he'd joked and called it *high charisma stats*, whatever that meant. If the thing refused to land and decided to only attack them from the safety of the sky, which it probably would because it wasn't stupid, they would utilize the various weapons they had that could launch into the air and potentially hit a moving target, like a crossbow with explosive bolts, and some sort of small missile launcher that Paulo was in charge of. Among the three teams, they also had elementalists who could create ice. And just like the vicious winter spirits that were the most constant nemesis of hunters, ice elementalists could form and throw ice javelins or, potentially, freeze a target into immobility.

Essentially, de-wing the thing.

Last night after dinner, Thom and Nora had sat on an outdoor dining table, neither of them bothered by the evening chill. Thom had encouragingly, annoyingly, told her to attempt to shoot the devil down with lightning bolts. But for all she knew, a single spark was the equivalent of healing a body covered in third-degree burns. Lightning was likely not effective against a demon, anyway.

No. She couldn't risk even practicing her lightning magic, as Thom kept calling it. Not unless another healer showed up or if a handler transferred someone from another base, which was unlikely to happen. The only time Nora could remember being in the presence of another healer was during that mini-apocalypse in North Dakota when someone mistakenly accused a girl of being the devil's spawn and then *oops* suddenly actual devils and angels got involved.

Sigh.

As Nora's group walked, silent and scanning, forever scanning the skies and forest, Thom, at the head of the group, abruptly stopped in his tracks, one foot hanging in the air before stepping gently down onto sand.

Hand signals were taught in the academy's system, much like any military. Nora was only familiar with the North American signals. And right now, Thom was indicating for them to wait—hand held up with all fingers and thumb together, and that there was a demon—forefinger and pinky raised.

But there was nothing that Nora could see, hear, or smell. No movement, no growling, no sulfur. If she couldn't sense what he sensed... That meant Thom had a sixth sense when it came to demons.

The Hammer wasn't just kinda big and kinda strong, didn't just have deep wells of stamina.

Thom was a *blood hunter*.

Fabled to be born under the sign of the hunter—not

Orion but an unnamed hero from before Orion was invented—all it meant was he could sense, track, and hunt demons and spirits and angels and gods as well as, if not better than, otherworldly beings could sense, track, and hunt hunters. People like Thom were the reason hunters were called hunters.

It made him a target.

It made him dangerous.

Shit.

As Thom slowly reached behind his back for his war hammer, Nora's stomach rolled.

And then the radio crackled.

Demon.

Thom felt it in his bones—that insistent pull, that unscratchable itch—and frantic shouting over the radio confirmed where it was.

North, north of where they parked. Either the devil wasn't as lured to him as usual or it was heading to him from that direction.

Thom signaled for the others to ready their weapons, and the second he signaled for them to follow him, he heard the explosion.

Paulo and Nora screamed in response, colliding with one another as Nora stopped short. Black smoke billowed near to where they had parked—likely, one of their Humvees had exploded.

Fuck.

Thom turned to the others, made sure they were alright, then signaled for them to follow, skirting the hazard. His blood ran hot, the presence of the demon growing stronger. But he couldn't know if it was on the ground or in the sky. He signaled for the group to watch both.

"Rally west," a voice rasped over the radio. The voice sounded like Kizzy's. "West," the voice repeated.

"Kiz?" Thom said into the radio. "We're west–southwest from the explosion." He noted his surroundings. "There's a clearing within eyeshot. A dried-up lake, maybe?"

"Yeah, I know it. On my way."

"Just stay out of the clearing," Angie's voice called over the radio, hitting Thom with a wave of relief.

The broad dry lake bed was circled by forest, and a hunting stand stood sentinel at the forest edge. Angie and the four hunters with her were the first to arrive, followed by Kizzy. And that was it. Four more hunters, gone. This was the first time Thom had seen Angie even hint at distress.

"We can't keep doing this," Kizzy rasped at Angie. "If I hadn't had to retie my boot laces I wouldn't fucking be here right now."

"If it really is the Jersey Devil," Heather said, "then it's clever enough to avoid not only being photographed or filmed, but it's also avoided generations of hunters for over a hundred years." She frowned and slipped her crossbow strap off her shoulder. "I don't think we should be here. I think we need to leave it alone."

"And let it burn down cabins?" Paulo said. "It roasted an entire sixth-grade elementary class!"

Heather and Kizzy exchanged an unknowable glance, then Kizzy said, softly, "Maybe it just wants its land back. Maybe we should let it happen, let people figure it out for themselves that they need to disinhabit the forests, make it all nature reserves."

"We can't just let it kill people, Kiz," Thom said.

"I'm not saying I'm okay with that—"

"I know. No one is." He sighed, seconds away from packing it in himself. "Look, it's a demon for sure, and a powerful one, not a god. We can't know how old, how long it's inhabited these lands. But we're all here. We're ready this time. And that"—he turned to the clearing—"is where I'll lure it to us. To me. It may or may not know you'll all be ready to take it down, but I'll do what I can to hold its attention."

Nora, frowning deeply, said nothing.

Angie stood in quiet deliberation, her thick arms crossed over her chest. "Do it," she said, then looked across the group to Thom. Her strained eyes conveyed unspoken words, but he knew exactly what was left unsaid.

Do what you were hired to do.

From the safety of the forest and hidden by the shadow of night, Nora sat with Kizzy, whose lungs had been damaged by smoke and fuel fume inhalation. The other hunters were dispersed across the forest edge, all within weapon range of Thom.

It was possible that this plan was a disaster, that the devil-demon could sense them wherever they were. It was possible that at any moment, a fireball would consume them. And so Nora's heart pounded much too fast, her ears hot against the late autumn chill.

"I never tried to bring down anything from the sky," Kizzy said. "I can manipulate wind currents. Hypothetically, I could wreck a helicopter. But choppers aren't dragons—

they don't have minds of their own to quickly correct for turbulence."

Nora paused her healing light and pulled back her hand from Kizzy's chest. "Breathe," she instructed.

Kizzy did, and then nodded. "Better. Thanks."

Nora managed a small smile, then turned her attention back to Thom where he stood in the clearing, taunting the sky with insults like *What are you afraid of?* and *Come out here you witless lizard!* and *What's your damage?*

And the insults just kept coming.

You stay up in the sky 'cause you're just a big ol' airhead!

This is so bogus! I'm so stoked to kick your wannabe demon ass!

"At least he'll die having fun," Kizzy said, their tone tinged with worry.

"Yellooooooo?" Thom shouted at the sky. "Come on ya big poser! You wanna know where the beef is?" He pounded his chest like a gorilla. "*I'm* the beef!"

"Oh...my god," Nora said. "Thom...is...a giant dork."

Kizzy laughed. "No duh."

They chuckled together, but Nora halted her breath when over her and Kizzy's laughter, over the shouting drone of Thom's insults, came a deep, drawn-out windy gasp, like if one combined a jet engine with a vacuum.

By the time she heard the roar, it was too late.

Thom's eyes had been on the dark, overcast sky, so he hadn't seen the ignited forest until the sound of screams carried over the wind.

People, on fire, staggered from the forest edge toward

him, none of them getting far, succumbing to the flames.

"Run!" came a high-pitched scream in the distance, but the growing forest fire blinded the scene. "Run!"

Two silhouetted shapes sprinted towards him, and then bursting from the flames, a dragon.

Less scaly and more gangly than he had envisioned, the beast was about the size and height of a chubby giraffe. But that didn't make its glowing red eyes or long, sharp fangs less menacing. Its massive wings spread and flapped as it charged, giving it the appearance of great size.

It *was* the Jersey Devil, matching the historical drawing of an ugly winged quadruped.

Kizzy was fast, but the Jersey Devil was faster.

Thom's breaths deepened, and the grip on his war hammer tightened. Heat stung his ears and lips and eyes as his blood pressure rose, as his heart pounded against his ribcage. And as the beast let out a piercing screech, nearly snatching Nora in its maw, Thom sprinted forth in weaves, circling to the back of the dragon as it chased his friends. He had gathered enough speed to launch himself onto the beast's back, and with a swooping swing he landed his hammer onto the space between the beast's wings. With a squeal and an abrupt halt, the beast threw Thom from its back, and his hammer was torn from his grip.

The last sound he heard was Nora, shouting his name.

Nora's scream brought her the attention of the dragon, taking it away from Thom where he lay on the ground. The growing forest fire on the other side of the clearing illuminated the scene.

The dragon roared and tried to take flight, but only its right wing rose while the left wing flinched. It tried again, failed again.

The dragon couldn't fly.

And Thom was back on his feet.

Kizzy roared at the beast and blasted it with a jet of air, a distraction as Thom retrieved his war hammer. Nora, heart racing and lungs drawing in deep breaths, gathered all the energy within and around her until her palms prickled and burned and overloaded with electricity.

In the same beat that she screamed and let loose the lightning magic at the dragon, Thom leapt onto the beast and brought his hammer down onto the other wing's joint. And then the demon's neck. And then its head. Its eye. Its snout. Its skull. Its brain.

Nora lowered her arms, her energy spent, and watched transfixed as Thom was painted again and again by the dragon's dark ichor each time he brought his hammer down, as he became not Thom but some violent creature, his long blond hair dripping purple-black, his form near indistinguishable from the dark of night.

Nora backed away from the scene, back toward the edge of the forest not on fire. She sat on a step leading up into an old hunting stand and tore her gaze from Thom to instead watch Kizzy approach the fire with arms raised almost as if to embrace the flames. They then lowered their arms, slowly, inch by inch. Kizzy repeated this movement, each time moving in closer to the dying flames until the forest fire was nothing more than embers. And then they collapsed to their knees.

Nora ran to Kizzy, hoping she had the energy to heal them should they pass out. But they didn't, at least not yet, and they walked together to the hunting stand, giving the ex-dragon and Thom a very wide berth.

From the step of the hunting stand, leaning against each other for comfort and warmth, Nora and Kizzy watched as Thom continued to mutilate the dragon's corpse with his hammer.

"Don't worry," Kizzy said. "His rage will drop soon."

"Rage?"

"That's what he calls it. Raging. Like 'roid rage. Except he doesn't need steroids. He just needs to get angry."

'*Are you asking if I could hurt you?*' Thom's question the night they talked over tea hit differently now.

"It's like those ancient warriors," Kizzy continued. "Berserkers. Same idea. Maybe even the same thing."

"Blood hunter," Nora said, and Kizzy didn't correct her.

When Thom fell to all fours, Kizzy said, "There, see? He's coming down. He'll be normal in a minute. Whatever normal is for him after a fight like this."

Nora swallowed the lump in her throat. "Will he hurt us?"

"Thom? Never. Not unless you're a demon or fallen angel or something." Kizzy eyed her. "Did you know you could create lightning before tonight?"

She nodded. Kizzy turned away, their attention back on Thom.

The clearing was silent, not even a breeze to rustle the evergreens and ashes around them. So when Thom began to sob in great, rolling heaves, there was nothing for Nora to do but cry, too.

Again. He had failed them all *again*.

How many more had died? Thom had seen Nora and Kizzy. Were they the only survivors?

The fire. The bodies.

Angie—gone. Paulo—gone. Heather, Vanessa...

Twelve. Twelve more hunters burned alive by a *fucking demon*.

And for what? What was the purpose of its rampage, this Jersey Devil? How much forest did it need for itself? Did it loathe humanity that much?

Why *now*?

Why the *fuck* had it avoided him to instead attack the others? Was it a simple matter of the creature being more intelligent than others he had battled? He was supposed to be the fucking bait for fuck's sake!

None of it made sense. It never did. Demons and devils raged and tricked and schemed, gods and angels looked on with amusement. And it just kept happening, over and over. To what end? How many more hunters, how many more people would he fail?

What was the point of it anymore?

Sitting on the ground, Thom curled into himself, wrapped his arms around his torso, every bit of him covered in inky gore. Snowflakes fluttered down, sticking to his arms before melting. The world was so dark now, dark and desolate. He wouldn't have been able to see a godforsaken thing were it not for his heightened senses.

There was only one bright side to this wretched moment.

The demon was dead.

His contract was fulfilled.

And he could leave.

"We should burn it," Nora said of the dragon's puddle of a corpse. "We can't just leave it here."

Kizzy turned to her, mild surprise raising their brows. "You've never fought a corporeal fire demon, have you."

Before Nora could ask what they meant, the dark mass that was the Jersey Devil erupted in purple flames. Thom stood, arms out to his sides as he, too, lit up in purple flames, but gave no indication that he was in pain.

And then the Jersey Devil was no more, a cloud of ash settling onto a sandy dried lake bed.

"Winter spirits in corporeal form explode into ice or water vapor," Kizzy said flatly. "Devils and other hellish things, fire and ash. Others turn to sand."

"Right," Nora said with understanding. "Can't leave a trace."

Thom, cleansed of death but instead covered in ash, raised his head to the sky, eyes closed.

"Do you think anyone else survived?" Nora quietly asked Kizzy.

Kizzy didn't answer. Instead, they said, "We should probably go see if at least one of our Humvees is drivable. Come on, Sparks. You can light the way."

Nora was grateful that Kizzy offered to be the one to tell the handlers what had happened, because she hadn't even learned most of the dead hunters' names.

After her shower, she plodded to her dark, quiet, shared room, everyone fast asleep by the time she, Thom, and Kizzy arrived at the academy covered in ash and sand and sweat and sadness.

Newcomers like her stayed in the hostel until better arrangements could be made. Some people shared larger apartments while others lived off academy grounds, if they had a family or simply wanted to. But hunters tended to gravitate toward one another, either preferring academy life or coalescing in a neighborhood, sometimes creating communes or building a development of condominiums just for them.

Most hunters weren't assigned to any one location. They were free to live their lives unless under contract. Nora's father liked to ignore the fact that he was a hunter, but her mother, when she was alive, was an academy girl. For Nora, there'd always been a pull in two opposing directions, her heart wanting to effectively retire to the suburbs, her brain knowing that escape was futile.

Death was, truly, the only known escape. There was always something lurking in the shadows.

A gentle knock sounded at the door. Both her room and the hallway were dimly lit, but she recognized the broad silhouette.

Thom gave her a painted-on smile. His hair, she realized, was freshly shortened—it looked like it had been chopped off by a blender.

"Lady Elianora," he said in a quiet, wry tone. "I've been sent to collect you." He shoved his hands into his jean pockets. "Your private chamber awaits."

"Kizzy and I are right down the hall," Thom said as Nora set down her meager possessions in the entranceway of her studio apartment. "Names are on all the doors, so..." He knocked twice on the doorframe.

Nora pulled back the sole window's curtains. The ground's sparse lighting dimly illuminated the gentle snowfall, and she sat by the window on its small bench to watch it.

She hadn't said a word since they left that clearing. Not to him, not to Kizzy, not when they checked for survivors, or when they drove back without any. He couldn't know her mind, couldn't know which part of the day's tragedies troubled her the most. But guilt gnawed, and he worried that from his actions, from his failures, he had destroyed any chance he might have had at...

Hell, who was he kidding?

"You cut your hair," Nora said, finally, her voice unsteady, looking him square in the eye for the first time since the demon attacked.

Her words pulled him in from the hallway. Leaving the door open, he took a seat on her desk chair, maintaining a distance between them.

"You look like"—she cocked her head—"a buff Billy Idol."

He laughed. "Wish I could sing like Billy." He swept a hand over his haphazardly shorn and unstyled tresses. "Yeah, I dunno. My head felt heavy."

She smiled, but it faded quickly. "You really frightened me, earlier."

He looked at his feet. "I can understand that."

"I never even asked if you were injured."

"I'm not injured," he said, careful to not lie and say that he was fine.

She stood from the small bench and approached him,

tentatively cupped his face between her palms, and looked down at him with a tilted expression that conveyed pity. With a slight swoon, she closed her eyes. Her brow furrowed first in concentration and then, clearly, from pain. Her tight lips slipped into a trembling frown, and as the warmth of her healing magic soothed the headache he had been bearing, she broke down into tears.

"I...couldn't...save them," she said between rolling sobs. "None of them."

She folded in on herself and Thom grasped her waist, leading her to her bed. He grabbed the Kleenex box that used to be Talia's.

Nora ignored the box of tissues and instead wiped her nose on her sweatshirt cuff. "What the hell good am I?" she asked.

Thom, sitting next to her, couldn't help but let out a small, weary laugh. "About as much good as I am."

Nora quieted, and they sat there together in sorry silence, watching the snow until Thom found the courage to say, "I'm sorry that I frightened you. I frighten myself, sometimes."

She sniffled and finally blew her stuffy nose. "It just reminded me of someone. He used to scare me a lot."

"Was he a blood hunter, too?"

She shook her head.

When she said nothing further, he said, "So, you've heard of people like me."

She nodded. "I didn't know you could get real violent, though. I guess it's true what the books say, that you're susceptible to silver and you've got demon blood in you?"

He winced at that. "Yeah, though the silver thing is more like an allergy. Just can't wear silver jewelry. Unfortunately, the blood part's true. It's something I've had to work on. But if it makes you any less afraid, I've never hurt anyone I actually liked."

"But could you? It looked as if you completely lost control, pulverizing that dragon-thing."

He looked away from her, out at the snow-speckled night. His teeth pressed so tightly together he had to make a conscious effort to relax his jaw.

"I don't know if I would ever completely lose control," he said honestly. "I can only promise that I never have, and that I'd sooner volunteer to get a root canal than harm you."

She eyed him warily. "What happened to the healer before me?"

Her curve ball hit him square in the solar plexus.

"The Jersey Devil happened," he said, and dropped his gaze to his hands. "Maggie was one of the first hunters it killed." He clenched his fists. "And she was my sister."

"Sister? I didn't know you had family."

"I don't. Not—not really. Not anymore, anyway. She was my foster sister. My best friend. But once she was old enough to attend an academy, our foster parents kicked her out."

That frozen moment of Maggie leaving with a single, small suitcase, her dark-red curls bouncing as she ran from the house and into the taxi, was the clearest memory he had of her. Not the birthdays or the laughter, not learning about being a hunter, learning the history. Just the second worst day of his life. His brain liked to torture him like that.

"She lived here, at the academy," he said. "I hadn't known. I'd tried to keep in touch with her over the last couple decades, but she didn't really want much to do with me after she left home. And then about five years ago I lost track of her." He wiped the tears from his cheeks. "She died the week before I came here. And I used to think..." He laughed at himself, laughed through his tears. "I thought, fuck, if I'd only arrived a week earlier..."

He shook his head. "But now, now I know it wouldn't have fucking mattered. That thing avoided me. It knew. It fucking knew me, like I knew it. And I can't help but wonder how many other creatures out there will avoid me, too. I used to think I was a danger because demons and gods and things came at me all the time, have since I was a toddler. Now I wonder if I'm a danger because they use me as a beacon to find other hunters."

"I'm so sorry about your sister," Nora said, and his breath faltered as her hand grasped his. "Maggie, was it?"

He nodded. "Her real name was Margot." He reached for a tissue to dab his eyes and blow his nose.

"Margot..." Nora looked at the ceiling as if it held an answer to a question. "I like that name." She then turned to him with a smile. Small, but it was there. And then she looked away. At her feet, at the desk, at their joined hands before she pulled away.

"Are you and I okay?" he asked, despite being terrified of the answer. "I don't want you to be afraid of me. And I don't want to end up on the wrong end of your lightning magic."

Unexpectedly, she laughed. Just a little, through her nose. "I almost hit you with it tonight."

"You did?"

"It was just as you leapt onto the thing's back the second time, after you were thrown. While you were down, I'd thought..." The corner of her lips twitched in a stifled frown. But quickly her eyes were brimming with tears, and the frown happened anyway. Barely above a whisper, she said, "I thought you'd died."

A knock sounded at the open doorway. Kizzy, their poofy hair unbraided and picked out, looking like a crown. Their curious expression dropped quickly.

"Shit," they said, "did I just ruin a moment?"

Nora laughed wearily. "No. It's okay. Come in."

Thom opened his arm for Kizzy to sit beside him. They entered, closing the door behind them before curling up at his side. Nora leaned her head against his shoulder, and he wrapped his arms around them both.

The three of them cried for those they had failed and, for Thom, those he had yet to fail.

Scars

THIS FUNERAL HAD been especially bleak. Too few people were in attendance for so many hunters having departed. There was no reception afterward, either. Just one joint service, a few words of encouragement, and the announcement of the academy's new principal handler, Simeon, replacing Angie.

The vibe in the academy had shifted between several days ago and now. When previously Thom had been the center of attention, the target of flirting and ogling and unwanted touching, now he felt all but shunned. And he couldn't help but assume that if he had only broken protocol and gone rogue to hunt the Jersey Devil alone, he would still be shunned, but all these needless deaths could have been avoided.

And so, as he read a new, unsigned contract on his desk, he wondered if he shouldn't just walk away from this life and return to how it used to be: a lonely half-starved vagabond, seeking shelter and company wherever he could, earning his keep however he could, moving on the moment he had outworn his welcome.

No matter where he went, it was clear now that he had to leave.

"Knock, knock," Nora said at his open doorway.

Her voice relaxed him, somewhat.

"Who's there?" he answered playfully, not looking up

from the contract.

"A sad sack dressed all in black."

He looked up that time. Unlike him in his warm and comfortable sweatpants and a hoodie, Nora was still wearing her funeral garb: black jeans, a black crop-top sweater, and her black leather jacket. She had even left her smoky eyeliner and crimson lipstick.

He slid a folder over the contract. "*Sadness*," he said woefully as he walked to his window, opening it and reaching outside for his secret stash. "Are you a *suffer through sobriety* sad sack, a *drown your sorrows in scotch* sad sack, or a *numb your worries into oblivion with vodka* sad sack?"

Nora let out a sad laugh. "Vodka, please and thank you." She snatched the bottle from him, unscrewed the top, closed her eyes, and sipped from the bottle. With her first swallow, she melted into herself. "Ugh, marry me."

Thom chuckled. "Sure. One day." Nora shot him a scrutinizing look, but he grinned and shrugged. "Maybe buy me dinner first."

She made a face, but otherwise ignored his comment, sat on the edge of his bed, and drank more. "Whatcha doin'?" she asked, nodding at his desk.

He had decided to hide his plans from Nora until they were finalized, but he couldn't bring himself to lie to her sad but hopeful face.

"I get requests sometimes," he said, sitting beside her. "Contract proposals sent to my current handler."

"Oh?" She sipped the vodka again. "You're, like, headhunted?"

"Yeah, pretty much. This one's for a job up in Toronto."

Nora frowned at him. "So...that's it? Slay and split?"

"Yeah. Exactly. They don't want me around anymore."

"Sure they do."

He had to look away from her soft blue eyes. "They blame me. I can feel it."

"For what? You didn't summon the demon-dragon."

"No. But I was meant to hunt it, to lure it right to me. I can't... I don't know if I should sign any more contracts. I don't know if I should be around others anymore."

"So, what, you'll just fuck off? Become a hermit?"

"Yeah. Maybe."

Nora glowered at him. "I think you're overreacting."

"People *died*, Nora. A *lot* of people died."

"That's not your fault. None of it's your fault."

"Isn't it? I should have just gone out by myself. All I had to do was smack it with my hammer."

"You said it yourself that it avoided you. It might still be out there were it not for me and Kizzy running it straight to you, you're welcome very much."

Thom laughed, but shook his head. "I don't want to be the reason you, Kizzy, or anyone else gets hurt."

Nora stood from the bed, took his hand, wrapped his fingers around the neck of the vodka bottle, then held his face between her palms before kissing his forehead.

Smiling down at him, she said, "If I promise to never get hurt, will you stay?"

Goddammit.

He closed his eyes, took a deep breath. "Fuck," he muttered, completely demolished. "Yeah, alright. I'll stay."

"Good." She sat down beside him again. "Now *that's* settled, let's get *drunk*."

Snuggling on his bed, they drank vodka from the bottle while listening to Thom's favorite nighttime mix tape until life's edges softened. At some point, Nora's fingers intertwined with his, and fantasy slipped ever closer to reality.

"I don't like being sad," she said, and took another sip of vodka.

He brought her hand to his lips to kiss it, holding it there long enough to learn the softness of her skin.

"I don't want you to be sad," he said.

She turned her frown to him, her eyes brimming with tears again. "I think you could make me not sad." Whispering, she added, "I think I could love you and it scares me."

Her drunken honesty took him by surprise. Fueled by liquid courage, he held her square chin between his finger and thumb, then pressed his forehead to hers.

"I think you could destroy me," he said, his soul preemptively shattering. "If you died..."

"I'm still here." She kissed his brow, his cheek, his lips. "Here, now. So love me, now."

And so he did.

The sky was a clear bright blue as Nora and Thom ate Keebler Elf fudge sandwich cookies for breakfast with some of his fancy-as-fuck Perrier to wash it down.

They ate in his bed, naked, Nora sprawled across his broad torso. Thom was splitting the cookie halves apart, making a game out of it, the way one would with an Oreo: if the fudge stuck to the cookie half in his left hand, he had to answer a question, and his right hand meant Nora would.

When he broke apart the next cookie, the unfudged half snapped in half as it usually did. He ate the broken piece, and Nora snatched the rest out of his hand with her mouth, like a wolf.

It was Nora's turn to answer a question.

"So," Thom began, "where did this gnarly scar come from?"

As he asked this, he grazed a feather-light touch along the length of Nora's left side where a scar stretched from ribs to hip. She shivered at his touch and squirmed, and he stopped his teasing to eat another cookie.

"So, I was seventeen," she said, "and me and my boyfriend at the time were home from the academy and having a snowball fight with childhood friends, none of them hunters. All of us were basically high on shrooms and pot that entire winter break—I mean, whatever, it was the seventies—and Vern and I forgot that it was the solstice."

"Uh-oh," Thom said, his dry and almost jaded tone indicating he knew exactly where this story was headed.

"The other kids had no idea why the date mattered, so when it started to snow—*on the solstice*—no one, including me and Vern, paid any mind to it, didn't have any weapons or anything silver, and when the Snow Maiden showed up I just thought I was having a bad trip."

"Big uh-oh."

"Short story shorter, I was nearly sliced in half by Father Winter's massive claw ripping down my side. Couldn't heal all of it. Too many fractured ribs." She grazed her palm against the eleven-year-old scar.

"The other kids were frantic," she continued, "screaming and crying and running for help. But as soon as they left the area, as soon as the battle was over, it was like it'd never happened for them. Even those who hadn't run away wondered why it was suddenly snowing and why I was covered in blood and why my boyfriend was carrying me, wrapped in his winter coat, to his car."

Vern had later yelled at her for bleeding on his car's upholstery, but Nora kept that little anecdote to herself.

Thom was eyeing her curiously. "You didn't know spirits could do that? To memory?"

"I know that *now*." Nora smacked the side of Thom's muscular ass, making him jump and laugh. "But back then I'd only been at the academy for a few months."

"I had all that stuff grilled into me by my foster parents."

"Good for you," she said, snatching a cookie and biting off the elf's head. "My parents mostly taught me how to drink and yell at baseball players on TV."

She fed the elf's feet to Thom, then ran a fingertip along one of the linear scars on his chest.

"Funny thing about scars," she said, then teased another one on his arm that had been dealt by something with wolf-sized claws. "A lot of people—non-hunters, mostly—want to hide them or buy expensive creams to fade them. They want to forget. But I can't heal scars away. Energy manipulation can only ask the body to heal itself by increasing blood flow or collagen production, kill bacteria. I can turn a wound into a scar, which means that scars aren't something that need to be healed. They are as they should be, a part of that person and their life. Scars are stories written across the skin."

Thom leaned forward to kiss the little scar on her shoulder, just a nick leftover from an encounter with Vern.

"So, how did you kill Father Winter?" Thom asked.

Nora frowned, then curled up close to him, wrapped herself around him. "We didn't. I would've died that day, I think, but right after I was ripped apart and thrown like a ragdoll by that frozen douchebag, one of those kids I thought wasn't a hunter tore the Snow Maiden apart just by clenching his fists. Water elementalist."

"No way."

"Yeah way. I didn't have it in me to ask questions, you know, on account of me bleeding out. I just remember him going into some kind of rage, then he..." She frowned. "He went quiet. Everything went quiet." She nuzzled into the crook of Thom's neck. "That boy, Travis, he died. Crushed. It was like those fuckers targeted him. Then Father Winter nearly gave us all frostbite with the blizzard he turned into."

Thom kissed her forehead and traced designs across the canvas of her back. "I'm really glad you survived," he said.

"That's what I do best," she said, touching her fingertips to her cheek, the one Vern had smashed not even a month ago. "But I'm tired of just surviving." She propped herself up on her elbows and planted a firm kiss on Thom's lips.

He grasped her waist and urged her onto her back, then let out a loud moan when she reached down and gave him a jump start with a burst of warm energy.

He laughed, and said, "Thank you, by the way, for not commenting on the fact that I am, indeed"—he looked down the length of his body—"not half-dragon."

Nora burst out in laughter. "Who'd have thought that *none* of the rumors about 'The Hammer' would be true."

He grimaced. "None of them?"

"Eh, I like that you're just some guy."

His eyes smiled down at her when he asked, "Some guy you could love?"

"Yeah," she said, smiling in return, keeping her fears to herself, instead tickling him with tiny, delicate sparks.

Leaves

NORA AND KIZZY huffed and puffed on the cold, leaf-covered ground, the short swords they had been training with at their sides.

The sound of weapons clanging and hunters grunting and laughing carried across the field—early mornings were for training.

Thom had been wrong about the others being angry with or disappointed in him. They weren't angry—they were afraid. And because they were afraid, even weeks after the Jersey Devil went down, they were hesitant to train with him despite wanting very much to do so when he'd first arrived. But Kizzy seemed to trust him implicitly, which made it easier for Nora to stop expecting him to flip on her like Vern always had. The last few weeks with him at her side and in her bed had been bliss.

It was fun, though a bit futile training with Thom. Demons and spirits rarely carried weapons—they had to take corporeal form to do so—and instead used elemental or energy manipulations to attack. But silvered weapons were an effective defensive tactic in any situation, corporeal or ethereal, and Thom's intention was to make sure Nora and Kizzy, as elementalists, weren't slacking in their weapons training.

By the time the sun neared its zenith, Nora's arms were

leaden and her head was throbbing. Kizzy, equally spent, used their elemental skill to create a breeze, making it slightly easier to breathe. Jealous, Nora used her own manipulations to 'heal' her aching muscles—it helped ease the ache of muscle fatigue in her forearms, but added to her overall exhaustion. She repeated the move on Kizzy's arms, though.

Thom—that asshole—checked his watch then leaned on his massive war hammer. "It's only been two hours," he said.

"The demons can have me," Nora drawled dramatically. "I'm pooped."

"I'm good, bud," Kizzy said. "I just wanted one more humiliating training session to remember you by."

"I can't believe you're leaving for Toronto," Nora said.

"Thom chickened out, so they needed *someone*."

Thom rolled his eyes and, with a frustrated huff, plopped onto the ground next to Kizzy. "You better write," he said.

"I'll send you a postcard," they said with a dimpled grin. Then, elbowing Nora, they added, "I'll address it to both of you."

Nora couldn't hold back her smile. "Thom, we're both tired. We need to rest up for tomorrow's party."

"I'm not staying up all night just because it's Halloween," he said. "I'll be there—of course I will. But then I'm out by ten."

"Wow," Kizzy said with a laugh, "you really are an old man in a young man's body."

"Nah, he's just asocial," Nora said.

Kizzy whipped up a gust of air to push at Thom's chest, forcing him to catch his backward fall with an arm. But he play-acted that he was injured, and reached out dramatically to Nora.

"Healer!" he rasped, but had a terrible poker face. "Avenge me!" Then he rapidly said, "Use your lightning magic that you should probably be practicing with so that it becomes easy to use when you need it ahhh*hhhggg*..."

And then The Hammer succumbed to his injuries.

Woe.

"He's kinda right, though, Sparks," Kizzy said.

Nora shook her head. "I've never heard of anyone who could create energy like that. Why do you think that is? Where are these people? I can't have everyone knowing. I worry they'd lock me away or kill me. It's bad enough my old handler probably suspects it."

Kizzy screwed their lips. "Yeah, I can see your point. Maybe not other hunters, but imagine what the electric companies would do if they knew people like you existed. They'd CIA your ass away."

"Right. I don't want any attention on me. From anyone."

"Well," Thom said, rising from the dead, "that's too bad, because lately you're all anyone seems to care about." He stealthily indicated with a nod behind Nora and Kizzy.

Stretching, Nora peeked over her shoulder and clocked half a dozen people—the same bunch who once fantasized over Thom's future children—standing not too far away with their arms crossed and faces soured.

"They're out for blood," Thom joked—hopefully joked.

"At least they stopped groping you randomly," Kizzy said.

"That's one positive of people thinking I'm a monster."

"No one thinks you're a monster," Nora said, despite not actually knowing if it was true. "And even if they did, hunters don't exactly shy away from monster fucking."

"That's just stuff that happens in paranormal romance novels," Kizzy said.

Nora raised a brow at Kizzy.

"I mean," they said, "I would think. If I read that kind of thing. Which I totally don't."

"They totally do," Thom said to Nora, and Kizzy shot another gust at him. Laughing, he added, "You do, though!"

"I fucked a shapeshifter once," Nora said, and the others paused their play fighting to gawk at her. She shrugged. "What? Wouldn't you be curious about sex with someone who could change parts of their body at will?"

Thom was blushing.

"Aren't shapeshifters demons?" Kizzy asked.

"No, they're closer to angels than anything else. And not all demons are bad. Case in point, Thom, with his demon blood. And I've dated hunters who were far worse than some demons I was hired to kill. Hating something just because of what it is isn't my thing."

Thom's stunned expression shifted into a delighted smile. "Look at you," he said proudly, "all progressive and supporting otherworld rights."

Nora toed his shin with her boot. "Come on. Let's go inside, make hot cocoa. We can watch *Poltergeist* and make fun of it."

Kizzy's Awesome Halloween / Going Away Party

SUBWOOFERS WEREN'T EXACTLY Thom's thing.

Neither were flashing lights, crowds, or loud anything. Likely, his heightened senses were to blame. It was also possible that Kizzy was right and he really was an old man at heart.

He watched Nora, Kizzy, and their friends dance from the lighting tech platform where it was safer, darker, quieter, and where only three other people chilled until the music shifted moods and they had to implement the next lighting sequence.

Thom had organized Kizzy's going away party that doubled as the academy's annual Halloween bash. The food, the drinks, the sound and light crew...everything except for the playlist and the DJ—that was all Kizzy. Thankfully his few friends, which included the lighting and sound crew, wouldn't need him around when he ducked out early.

He stood in the shadows, but Nora and Kizzy knew where he was and waved to him as they bounced in sync to The B-52's "Love Shack" then shouted the lyrics to each other. Then they insistently waved him over. After a deep breath and a groan no one in that gymnasium could hear, he slipped through the railings of the balcony and jumped the short height to the waxed wood floor. Before he knew it he was embarrassing himself completely, singing and clapping and 'dancing' along with Nora and Kizzy and everyone else.

Why exactly had he decided to remain sober tonight?

As Kizzy danced, their silver-purple faerie wings strapped to their back fluttered, and their green glittery make-up and dress caught the flashing lights, making them sparkle. Nora, like Thom—and unlike most people on that dance floor—was dressed in whatever nice-enough clothing she had available but had shed her jacket, which was safely tucked away with the lighting crew.

As "Love Shack" crossed over into When In Rome's "The Promise," Kizzy strained to look up to Thom and said something he couldn't hear over the gym's cacophony. He bent down to them and heard *I'm gonna miss you*. Standing up straight, he grinned down at the person who had become so close so quickly after he arrived earlier in the year, and couldn't fight the urge to wrap his arms around them in a dizzying spin-hug. When Kizzy's feet touched solid ground again, he held them to him tightly, careful not to crush their wings.

"The universe better treat you like goddamn royalty," he shouted into their ear.

Kizzy tipped up on their toes to kiss his cheek, and then swept Nora in for a group hug.

"Kizzy!" someone shouted and grasped their shoulder. "Come!"

Kizzy smiled back at him and Nora, and then scampered off into the night to do glittery faerie things.

Nora wrapped her arms around his neck, no longer dancing in time to the song, just sort of swaying.

Olive juice, she mouthed. Or maybe, just maybe, it was *I love you*.

Thom leaned in to kiss her, and they swayed together as pinks and purples and greens flashed around them, and the music and whooping and laughter faded into the background.

He hoped Nora could sense it through his kiss that he was desperately, painfully in love with her. But just in case she didn't, he spoke it in her ear, the same words he had once said platonically to Kizzy: "Darling, I love you, I love you, I love you."

"The Promise" crossed over into "Sweet Dreams (Are Made Of This)" by Eurythmics, and it was after ten o'clock but—fuck it—he wasn't tired and Nora was here, swaying in time to his favorite song, giving him the sexiest smoky *fuck me* eyes he had ever seen. He took her round face between his palms and kissed her briefly before giving in to the rhythm and letting his body move in whatever way it wanted to, which thankfully must not have been all that bad as Nora was smiling and doing the same.

Prince's "When Doves Cry" took over, and Nora danced closer, moving with him, sneaking kisses and love bites, squeezing his ass and not minding when he did the same to her in her tight black jeans. Madonna's "Express Yourself" and Salt-N-Pepa's "Push It" had him aching to whisk Nora away to his apartment, but she was clearly having too much fun.

AC/DC's "You Shook Me All Night Long" had them jumping and screaming the lyrics just as Kizzy re-emerged, wings fluttering in time to the music, only to disappear again into the crowd of hunters.

When the DJ put on Rick Astley's "Never Gonna Give You

Up," people booed, and the song was quickly replaced with Paula Abdul's "Cold Hearted."

"I actually like Rick Astley," Nora said.

"Yeah, me too."

After another hour of dancing, drinking, mingling, eating hors d'oeuvres, more drinking, going to the bathroom, fucking in the bathroom, and more dancing, he and Nora sat at the top of the bleachers, watching everyone else dance.

Nena's "99 Red Balloons" played out and crossed over into Journey's "Don't Stop Believin'," and they made out until Sting and The Police started crooning "Every Little Thing She Does Is Magic," because Thom couldn't stop laughing.

"What's so funny?" Nora insisted, laughing with him.

"Oh, just, everything. I swear I heard this song playing in my head the moment I met you. Like it was fate or something."

"Yeah, right."

"Yeah," he said softly. "Right."

T'Pau's "Heart and Soul" began to play, and he grasped Nora's waist to bring her onto his lap. The lights had shifted to a deep purple, haloing her messy low ponytail, giving her an otherworldly appearance.

As they kissed, his watch beeped, indicating it was now midnight. And right on cue, the ghosts appeared.

Nora heard light gasps of surprise. A smirk on Thom's face confirmed it was nothing bad, and when she sat at his side to look around the gym, she finally saw it: ethereal apparitions, silvery and delicate, had appeared throughout the hall.

"Is this why academies always hold parties on Halloween?" she asked.

"Didn't you go to an academy?"

"Yeah, but I didn't go to any social functions."

She had seen plenty of ghosts over the years, mostly weak and harmless energy residuals but others more worrisome entities. These ghosts—of all shapes and sizes, some nothing more than orbs and others looking like intricately projected holograms—hovered or stood still, wove between the dancers or flew around the high ceiling, and some even appeared to be dancing. Normally ghosts projected no light of their own; it cost them too much energy. But tonight, with the veil between worlds briefly breached, they shimmered under the purple lights.

"It's kinda beautiful," she said. When she looked at Thom, he was looking at her, eyes dark but sparkling from the purple lights. She kissed him and said into his ear, "Let's get outta here."

He eagerly jogged to go grab her jacket, still tucked away with the lighting crew. As she scanned the room for Kizzy, she couldn't find them in the electric-purple sea of figures, so she headed for the exit where she'd meet Thom.

"Heart And Soul" ended and, after a brief silence, Rick Astley's "Never Gonna Give You Up" came on again, and everyone, again, booed.

"VERY FUNNY!" someone shouted.

Unlike the last time, though, the DJ didn't cut the song short. The dancers stopped dancing, except for the few ghosts that continued, though not in time to the music, perhaps hearing a completely different song in the otherworld.

Nora tried to see across the gym to DJ Tuesday's setup, but he wasn't up on a stage and Nora was at most average in height.

"Here ya go," Thom said, handing her her leather jacket.

"'Bout time," she said, slipping it on. "Let's get outta here before he starts playing 'Lady In Red.'" She laughed at herself.

Thom stopped in his tracks to gawk at her. "You don't like Chris de Burgh?"

She shot him her best glare of disappointment. "You do?" He mirrored her expression. "That's it," she said, pushing the door open. "I want a divorce."

"Gotta marry me first, darling."

As the door slowly closed behind them, inside the gym someone screamed, something shattered, and the purple lights blinked out.

"Never Gonna Give You Up" kept playing until it got stuck with a loud scratch, looping back, again and again, repeating the titular line.

Thom sensed it the moment someone screamed. "It's demons," he said to Nora.

"Shit. Do you think the Jersey Devil can reincarnate that quickly? Maybe we just pissed it off." She reached inside her left boot to pull out a dagger.

"You're carrying too," he said, impressed.

"Always." She waited for him to reveal his own dagger, and when he did, she shot him her cocky smirk. "I knew I married you for a reason."

He chuckled and held open the gym door for her. "Not married yet, darling."

The gym echoed with screams and shouts and chaos, and several hunters ran outside. Inside, some held colored glow sticks or wore glow jewelry, while others flashed their elemental magic, but it wasn't enough to see what was happening. The doors shut behind them as Nora maintained a gentle golden glow in her palm to light their way and look for something along the wall.

A light switch. It didn't work.

"I can't hold this forever," she said of her orb.

When Thom tried to push the double doors open again to let in some light, they wouldn't budge. "What the hell? They're stuck."

Thom kicked them, and the rebound off the unmoving doors hurt his leg and knee.

A scream—shrill, and laced with pain. Nora dispelled her orb, and Thom's eyes strained in the dark. Almost seeing hurt more than not seeing at all.

He couldn't recall many times he had been truly frightened. He had been in so many sticky situations that, after a while, he stopped breaking a sweat. But now, he was truly terrified.

Nora reached for his hand and clutched it just as someone bumped into him, rending them apart again. Someone screamed, something thudded and scuffed the floor, someone groaned, someone stepped on his toes, and an elbow prodded his abdomen.

Terror was slowly winning over his resolve, and he couldn't help but think: if only he had left by ten. But then Kizzy and Nora would have been here without him. And if something had happened to them...

"Nora!?" he shouted.

In response, her golden magic flashed. "Here!"

She was on the floor, all but being trampled. He pulled her to her feet and held her close, turning his back to the gym, hoping to use his body as a shield to protect her.

"What's going on?" Nora asked, loud enough to be heard over the screams and over Rick Astley, who kept repeating the same titular line until the scratching record narrowed in on a single word.

You—*scratch.*

You—*scratch.*

You—*scratch.*

You—*scratch.*

He didn't know what was going on. He didn't like not knowing.

Then, all at once, everything flipped—the gym flashed a blindingly bright lavender, the music screeched to a halt, everyone's screams peaked and dimmed, and the crowd stood still where they were. The light that filled the hall faded, and soon the only light source was a deep violet flame around the DJ's turntables.

A dark, tall, lean figure emerged from those flames, walking as if a model on a catwalk, its long legs showing off. As it walked, the figure left a trail of purple flames.

The figure was walking straight for Thom.

As it neared, he could just about discern a face: human, rectangular with strong features, days' old scruff across its jaw and neck, and brown curls on its head. Most unsettling, however, was the fact that its pale flesh—and it was indeed in corporeal form—became disfigured the closer it walked, having the appearance of being burned or, Thom thought, struck by lightning, with a forked trail of dark lines crossing its face and neck.

The demon grinned. An awful, wicked expression that knew too much. Even its eyes were saying something sinister. Those pale eyes, once a shade of blue, blanched as it encroached.

And then Thom realized—it wasn't grinning at him.

"Norrraaa," it crooned in an almost feminine, mellifluous voice, slowly tilting its head to the side as if inspecting her. "How lovely it is to see you again. I hope you enjoyed my little attempt at a Rick Roll."

Thom frowned in confusion. No one said a word.

"What, too soon?" The demon pouted. "Oh, yes. Much too soon. That joke will make sense in about 20 years."

Nora appeared petrified by fear, eyes wide and body stiff. But her fists, he noticed, sparkled with electricity.

"You're not him," she said.

"No," it said wistfully, "I'm not. You killed Vern. You watched him die, watched him *cook*." It delicately drew its fingertips across its face scarred with purple-red tendrils. "That's what drew me to you. Your pain and your vengeance. Your *hatred* and your *fear*."

It spoke those words with such malicious fervor that it made Thom's skin crawl.

Nora killed someone?

The demon laughed. "Vern's soul welcomed me in like a black hole." It shot Nora an open-mouthed smirk bordering on a snarl. And then he pouted, mocking. "He wasn't a very good boyfriend, was he?"

"Shut up," she growled, and her sparks grew brighter.

"I'm glad you're enjoying that power. That...*spark* of freedom."

"Shut *up!*" Nora shouted, and lightning shot to the floor

from her clenched fists. The crowd gasped in response.

The demon's snarl grew, and with a flick of its wrist, Nora's lightning magic was snuffed out and she went flying toward the demon faster than Thom could react.

"Vengeance demon!" he shouted, knowing this beast, naming it.

Around the gym, elementalists briefly flared their varied magic—a flicker of flame, a shimmer of ice, a rush of wind. But Nora was in the demon's grasp, too close for wanton attacks.

"The Hammer," the demon said through a laugh, finally acknowledging him, almost jadedly. "You've been enjoying playing with—what did your little friend call her?" It gazed into the darkness before meeting Thom's gaze again. "Sparks?"

In an instant, the dagger that Nora carried was at her throat, held by her own hand but, clearly, given the terrified look in her eyes and the tears streaming down her cheeks, not by her own volition.

"Don't you fucking hurt her," Thom said, his voice low with building rage.

"You can feel it, can't you," the demon said to him. "That pull from deep within. The urge to let go, to destroy, to...savor."

"FUCK OFF," someone shouted from the darkness.

Thom's heart raced. Fast, much too fast. Blood rushed to his fingertips and ears, and his vision sharpened.

The gym was dark aside from the purple flames around Nora and the demon. As it laughed, a glittery faerie flashed behind the flames before disappearing again into the darkness.

"What do you want with her?" Thom growled at the

demon.

"Her?" The demon cackled. "I don't want *her*."

Your fault, a voice sounded in his head.

Your fault. Sharp, like an ice pick to the eye.

Your fault.

Your fault.

Your fault.

Your fault.

Your fault.

Your fault.

Your fault.

Your fault.

Your fault.

Your fault.

Your fault.

Shimmering in the flames, ethereal figures materialized. Slowly, some of the shades became recognizable.

Paulo.

Vanessa.

Heather.

Angie.

And Maggie.

"Stop it," Thom ordered the demon, his heart hammering.

"Ohhh, *stop it*, he says," the demon teased as more figures formed out of the flames. "So convincing." It turned to Nora. "You *like* this guy?"

One of the figures slipped through the darkness and was in front of Thom, swinging its arm with a deathly cold touch. Thom flinched and yelped, and a thrust of his dagger dissipated the shade.

Others around him screamed, but he could barely see

their attackers.

Your fault.
Your fault.
Your fault.
Your fault.
Your fault.
Your fault.
Your fault.
Your fault.
Your fault.
Your fault.

"*Rrraaage* for me, blood hunter!" the demon shouted. "Give me a taste before I end you."

Something cold tickled Thom's neck, and he swatted it away. "You want a taste?" he shouted, and shot the demon a snarling grin. "BITE ME."

Someone near him screamed then grunted, and the swoosh of a weapon cut air—others had brought blades to this party. An air elementalist sent a gust at the demon, but the attack barely made it falter and instead the demon used whatever telekinetic power it possessed to throw the hunter further away into the darkness, only known by the person's subsequent scream and the faraway crash of their body. Ice, formed by other elementalists, crept up the demon's neck and face, but someone met a similar fate—a terrible scream, a crash, a groan.

Thom swiped at the shades that kept coming for him, rising from the otherworld as if summoned.

Your fault.
Your fault.
Your fault.
Your fault.

Your fault.
Your fault.
Your fault.
Your fault.
Your fault.
Like bees, small ice-cold shades swarmed him, searing his cheek and elbow and shin with a touch, and another scratched through his shirt and into his chest. He and a student cut through the shades, sending them back to the otherworld, but he was left in severe pain and shivering.

Five shades surrounded him now, all of them resembling those who had fallen to the Jersey Devil. Maggie, screaming at him, her hair no longer curls but coils of snakes, hissing accusations.

Your fault.
Your fault.
Your fault.
Your fault.
Your fault.
The shades multiplied again, scattering the hunters who had been fighting them off, and the cold grip of death wrenched the dagger out of Thom's hand. Someone at his side screamed, but a spirit forced him to look toward Nora, the otherworldly grip on him as fierce as it was on her.

My fault.
My fault.
My fault.
My fault.
My fault.
Screams all around him. Except from Nora.

Nora, whose wide, terrified eyes were fixed on him.

Nora, whose tears reflected the cold purple light of the

otherworld as she mouthed, *Olive juice.*

That same light reflected a glittery faerie creeping out of the darkness, carrying a silver-plated sword.

"Nora," Thom rasped as icy tendrils wrapped around his heart. "Nora," he said again.

His eyes burned.

"Make..."

The room grew bright.

"...Sparks..."

He couldn't feel his fingers.

"...Fly."

As Nora screamed his name, stars of every color filled his vision.

Thom closed his eyes and embraced release, a burden no more. And then sunlight haloed two loving smiles—the very first souls he had failed.

Nora's scream accompanied crackling electricity that cloaked her entire body, heating the dagger forcibly held at her throat, burning her.

The demon lurched away from her with a yelp, then from the darkness a sword sliced through the air at the demon's chest, deeply wounding it. Silvery ice quickly encased the corporal fiend's ankles and wrists, causing it to fall, weighted, to its back. Behind it, shimmering against the purple flames stood Kizzy and other elementalists, hands raised and teeth bared.

"Now!" Kizzy shouted.

A dozen hands slammed down, and a great thunderous clamor echoed throughout the gym.

Nora's heartbeat thumped in her ears, and she still couldn't move from where she stood. But the demon, too, seemed frozen in place, and it gasped for air.

Kizzy broke from the line of elementalists to approach the demon, sword in hand and faerie wings fluttering. They pointed the sword at the demon's face, inches away.

"Don't...*EVER*," they cried, "crash my *FUCKING* parties!"

With a collective scream from the hunters and demon alike, the ice cuffing the demon shattered along with its hands and feet, the air encasing it depressurized with a grotesque hiss, and Kizzy's sword pierced its throat with a swift left–right tilt and a final thrust, dismembering its crushed and shriveled head.

The demon's grip on Nora ended abruptly, and the dagger she'd been holding clanged against the floor. She dropped to her knees, and the cloak of lightning that had been tickling and prickling her entire body dissipated. Then the demon and all its pieces burst into icy purple flames, leaving no trace.

What this demon had wanted was unclear. It had taken the guise of Vern, wrecking Nora's constitution, but had done so to get to Thom. Why? Because Thom was a blood hunter? Why now? Because the veil between worlds was thin?

What had the demons said about her lightning? Had it...given her this power? Nora shook the thoughts out of her head. None of that mattered right now.

The gym's fluorescent lights flickered on, and the music recommenced in the middle of Richard Marx's "Right Here Waiting," but DJ Tuesday was nowhere to be found.

Nora knelt on all fours, Kizzy at her side, both of them catching their breath. At the other end of the gym stood a crowd of hunters and shadowy figures, all looming over something shielded from Nora's view.

"Thom!" Kizzy shouted and sprinted toward the crowd.

Time and pulse and breath slowed. The music stopped. Kizzy's words of *He isn't breathing* flew right by Nora where she stood next to onlooking hunters and benign ethereal ghosts, stunned as if such words could never have been spoken, as if all of reality had ceased and this display of panicked screams was a primetime movie, overacted for their entertainment.

Kizzy started chest compressions, alternating with a rush of air shoved in and out of his lungs by their manipulations, sparing them their own oxygen.

"Sparks!" they shouted. "Snap out of it and zap the man!"

Something cold brushed her hand, and looking down, Nora saw that it was a ghost, a purple shade her height, faceless but somehow known as a wordless, benevolent emotion. The shade's hand left hers to gesture at Thom's body where he lay, pale and devoid of life.

With a gasp, Nora knelt by Thom's side, shoved Kizzy's hands away, placed one palm over his heart and another at the other side of his torso, and let out a burst of lightning into his chest that thrust his body into a single violent convulsion.

Olive juice. The words hummed in Thom's mind.

A two-door garage, open to the driving rain and thunderstorm outside. A thousand jigsaw puzzle pieces spilled onto a card table. Quiet wordless music scratching over an old radio. Nora, in a short-sleeved purple top, smirking. Beside her, a faceless form, fitting a piece of blue sky into place as lightning flashed outside.

Olive juice.

Silver and pink trinkets dangling from a crib mobile. A halo of black hair framing a chubby, giggling face. A little one, taken in because she had no one else. The sunset light, reflecting against the silver-plated decorations of the crib.

Olive juice.

A whiteout blizzard, broken by fire. Evergreens bowing toward thunder. Nora, sword in hand, fighting alongside two women. Golden healing warmth surrounding a small faceless form. The sun shining in the blue sky, blinding-bright.

Olive juice.

"Goddammit Thomas," Kizzy shouted, "you are *not* allowed to die."

Nora sobbed as she shocked him again, then resumed compressions as Kizzy pushed and pulled air in and out of his lungs.

"Not yet," Nora swore to Thom. "Not yet, not yet. You don't get to go yet."

Weeks ago, when Vern had Nora's throat in his hands, when he almost ended her on the floor of their living room, no life flashed before her eyes. No regrets had taunted her, no hopes were dashed. There had been only a single emotion: pure, violent hate with a single brutal target. That hate had consumed her, and she in turn consumed hate, used it, relished it.

Now, using that same unexpected power, not caring

where it came from, a new emotion overcame her: pure, brutal love with a single devastating target. This love consumed her, and she in turn consumed love, accepted it, cherished it.

Kizzy's wind entered and exited Thom's lungs, raising and lowering his chest between Nora's steady compressions.

Around Thom gathered several shades, hovering as only ghosts could. They flashed hot lavender...and then they were gone.

With a stuttering sob, Nora released another pulse of energy. Thom's body convulsed again.

A cough. A groan. The audience gasped, and Kizzy fell to their knees across from Nora.

Thom wheezed loudly, and his breaths lobbed in and out. He coughed again, and his breaths came slow and heavy, but steady.

And then he opened his eyes. Those smiling, grey-green eyes.

"Hey, Healer," he rasped, giving Nora a tilted grin.

Nora smiled down at him, lightly brushing his shorn hair. "Hey, Hammer," she managed to say through her tears.

His fingertips lightly pressed to her cheek before he closed his eyes, and between heavy breaths, he said, "Marry me."

Nora laughed and kissed his forehead, temple, mouth. "Okay, maybe. Might wanna get you to the infirmary first."

"Smart," he said, and his lips twitched up.

And then, quiet.

Asshole

"I'M NOT ANGRY," said the new principal handler, Simeon, his large, dark hands folded on his desk. "After what happened, it's hard to be angry. But we have concerns. I'm sure you can understand. This is unfamiliar territory for all of us here. We will do our due diligence in researching the topic, but it would have been helpful if you had come forward about this...*talent*...sooner."

Nora couldn't look the man in the face. Not because she was ashamed, but because everyone these last few days looked at her as if she would break at any moment, either fall at their feet in tears or shock them to death. Pity and fear came at her from all sides, and Simeon's wizened face and thick grey eyebrows spared no emotion. All she wanted was to be left alone, to sit beside Thom where he lay comatose.

"Just don't send me away," Nora said, her voice scratchy from the constant crying. "I won't leave here. Not now."

"No one here is experienced in this kind of energy manipulation. You need to understand, I have the safety of students to worry about."

"I wasn't brought here to instruct students. I was brought here to help Thom with his contract, which was completed, which means my contract is completed." That time, she did look Simeon in the eyes, hoping her words hit home. "I'm not leaving if he's not leaving."

When Simeon swallowed his frown, she had to look away again.

"If you insist on staying," he said, "then you must help us in our research, until we can locate someone you can train with. There is no other way this can work. But if there is so much as a spark—"

"I won't do it," she insisted. "I don't want to. Don't want this. Just give me some downers—I'll be fine."

"The academy psychiatrist can arrange something."

Silence.

"I think Thom will be alright." He sounded so sure of himself. "They say he spoke to you, joked with you before losing consciousness."

Joke. Sure. A joke.

'Marry me...'

Asshole.

For days on end, Nora cried at Thom's bedside in the infirmary. Kizzy delayed their departure and cried with Nora, as did the few friends still living that Thom had made.

The nurses gave Nora a cot. People brought her food.

Lots, and lots, and lots of McDonald's. Someone even brought her a Happy Meal, in which was a cute Snoopy toy that she put on Thom's bedside table.

To pass the time, she slept most of the day, then watched television at night. She read a couple books Kizzy found and thought might be useful for Nora and her lightning—they weren't.

Why were the only descriptions of lightning creation in

fiction?

"Maybe it was stigmatized," Kizzy said, "so no one talked about it. There are some really old diaries in the library. Have to read them in the special documents room, though. With gloves on. You could go there. I'll stay here with Thom."

"I'm not leaving him."

"Okay..." Kizzy said through a sigh. "I wonder if a little zap would snap him out of his coma."

"I'd rather not try. Anyway, I healed him. Or, rather, felt around for something that needed healing. Other than a fractured sternum, he was fine." Nora frowned. "Maybe he's just tired."

Several days in, Nora and Kizzy's conversations turned to what exactly had happened at the party. The veil between worlds was always weak during those hours between the sunsets of Halloween and All Souls, but something in particular had called to that demon. Likely, that thing had been Thom, too attractive a target for the demon to ignore, despite him being surrounded by other hunters.

"Rage," Kizzy said. "They feed off of it. Maybe there was enough of it, in our world or theirs, to allow the demon to corporealize and give it enough power to control people." Eyeing Nora warily, Kizzy asked, "Did you really kill your boyfriend?"

"Yep. Yep I did. After he tried to kill me for wanting to leave him."

"Harsh."

"Yeah."

"It sounded like the demon gave you that lightning power."

Nora frowned at her hands where they lay limply on her

lap, then let a trickle of energy spark between her fingertips. "It doesn't feel evil."

"It could be, if that's what you were."

Nora let the electricity dissipate. "It doesn't seem to work like other manipulations. I think it's more like how elementalists form fire. It doesn't exactly come *from* me, but it also does, like an interaction. I feel something coming from me but I don't have lightning in me, they don't have fire in them. Something I release... I think it collects electricity around me then sends it back out."

"You should talk to one of the fire elementalists here. They don't create fire from nothing, for sure, just like I can't create an oxygen molecule, I can only shove it around."

Nora nodded, then played with another trickle of electricity. "Maybe all of this magic comes from the otherworld," she said softly. "Not evil, not good. Just...other."

"That's the popular theory, yeah." Kizzy stirred up a gentle whirlwind, rustling the papers at the top of Thom's chart. "But wouldn't it be nice to know for sure..."

One day, Thom's foster parents arrived. Why, Nora couldn't guess. He'd mentioned not having the best relationship with them, mentioned not having any real family anymore. But perhaps their information was in whatever file the academy had on Thom, and Simeon had phoned them, just in case.

In case...

Nora sat outside Thom's room, half-listening to their muffled voices speak about him as if they knew him anymore. What would those people do with his body, if he died?

Did Thom want to be buried? Burned? Where would he want to be interred? Where would he want his ashes released?

Nora tried to think of what he would have wanted, and decided against cremation. Thom didn't like being so scattered—he wanted a home, somewhere he could rest, be loved, be himself.

And that's what did it, what finally crushed her: she and Thom both wanted a home, stability, certainty. And maybe, just maybe, they could have created that together.

The Beginning

THOM WOKE TO the sound of Nora stuffing her face with a Big Mac.

He propped himself up just enough to watch her eat the entire thing in a matter of half a minute.

Impressive.

"Hope you brought enough for the class," he choked out, then lay back down on his pillow, exhausted.

"*Phm?*" she said through her full mouth, then ran to his side and cupped his face in her hands that smelled of burger and fries.

"Hey, darling." He gave her what he hoped was a smile. Why did it hurt to talk? And think? And breathe?

He didn't expect the frantic kisses Nora planted all over his face, didn't think them necessary. But he wasn't about to complain.

"Did you make the sparks fly?" he asked. "Considering you're alive, and I'm..." He checked his arm, noted the IV catheter stuck in his inner elbow. "I guess I'm alive, too. Please tell me you whooped that demon's ass."

Nora laughed and kissed him. "Shit," she said, and brought her McDonald's cup to him and tilted the straw. "Drink. It's been a while."

He did. He loved lemonade. He sipped again, then noticed Nora was crying.

"Was the fight that bad?" He tried to sit up, but his chest hurt. A lot. He looked down, pulled his hospital gown to the side—the center of his chest was yellow-brown with old bruising, and parts of his chest and abdomen were covered in gauze.

When he looked up again, Nora was folded in on herself, sobbing, and Kizzy was running into the room alongside a doctor.

There were dreams Thom recalled, flashes of false memories, like photographs. But having been in a coma for six days, it was likely he had many, many such dreams, probably influenced by those talking near him. Most of the dreams he remembered involved him hammering nails into wood with a regular hammer.

"I don't remember it," he said to Nora and Kizzy. "Dying. I just remember dreams. Or, maybe..." He didn't want to say it was a glimpse of heaven, but for all he knew, it was.

"You were gone for a few minutes," Kizzy said. "Doctor said any longer and you'd've been toast. And they couldn't even figure out why you were in a coma." They playfully smacked his shin. "Coulda just said you needed a nap."

"Hey. Be nice. I died."

He hadn't intended for those words to be upsetting, but Nora started crying again.

He gently rubbed his chest. "Guess I'm lucky I didn't leave the party early. If ghosts came after me and you two hadn't been around..."

Nora sobbed harder, then secluded herself in the bathroom, turning on the exhaust fan, camouflaging any other sound.

"If you're indebting your life to me," Kizzy said, "I can ask for you to be tacked on to my contract as my bodyguard." They smirked.

He huffed a laugh. "Actually...I think I'm done. No more contracts, no more academies."

"Not more of this cheesemongering nonsense."

"No, no. I'm thinking more like...general contractor. Landscaping? Something I can slip into with a bit of training. Maybe start up my own biz."

"And when the demons and spirits and ghosts show up while you're building someone's deck?"

He shrugged. "Keep a dagger in my toolbox."

Disappointment was written across Kizzy's thinned lips, but he could also tell that they understood he was serious.

"Fuck," they said. "Well, when you inevitably get bored, call me. And if you fall out of touch I *will* hunt you down."

"I would expect nothing less."

Nora emerged from the bathroom, red-faced but quiet.

"Hey, Kiz," he said, "can you—"

"Already gone." They kissed his forehead before leaving.

Nora sat on a chair by the side of his bed, arms folded over her waist, silently distressed, her gaze set on that disquieting middle space where worry and fear lingered.

"Lady Elianora..." He hoped that annoying her would help her smile. She looked up at him, at least. "Wouldst thou...do me the honor of, uh, sitting by mine—ah, hell, that's terrible. Nevermind." He sighed and, ignoring the aches in his body, sat up, slipped on his slippers, and walked all of two steps before Nora stopped him and made him sit back down.

"Not without the nurse," she said. "Baby steps,

remember?"

"Yeah, yeah." He groaned as he reclined against the angled bed. "Forget about me for a second. Are *you* okay?"

"Fuck off," she sputtered as she began to cry again, this time crawling into the bed to lay beside him.

"I'll take that as a not yet." And though it hurt a bit, he welcomed her head on his shoulder. "I don't remember everything from the fight. I remember the party, thankfully. And I remember thinking how so fucking in love with you I am."

"Shut up," she said through a mess of sobs and laughter.

"Nope. Can't shut me up, not about this."

When Nora stopped crying, he asked her about the fight. He wanted to hear it from her what had happened, and how he died. She held his hand as she spoke.

"This is all my fault," she said, voice quiet. "I killed Vern. I killed him with that lightning. It's why I came here in the first place. My handler covered it up. I'm literally a murderer and that demon knew it."

"Was this Vern fellow the reason you came here with a black eye?"

She sniffled. "Yeah."

"And I'll wager it wasn't the first time he gave one to you."

"Definitely not the first."

"Then fuck Vern. And fuck that demon for ruining Kizzy's party."

Nora sputtered out a laugh, then groaned. "Vern and I had been together since high school. When we were sixteen, we considered ourselves married. Then at the academy we lived together, and after that, too. It was like, common-law by then, married without the paperwork. I looked past it all during our time together, all the shit he pulled, the others he fucked, because I fucked other people too, did shit he wouldn't have liked, too. But stealing from me, hitting me, all the insults—I'd had enough, had to get out of there. He caught me packing my suitcase." She wiped her nose against the back of her hand. "He didn't want me leaving. Thought he owned me, or...was owed me."

"I hate that the demon used you to get to me."

"Yeah. Well. No good thing comes free."

Thom wanted to remind her that he wasn't any good, that he was dangerous, a demon magnet, and left nothing but death in his wake. But she would have just told him to shut up about it already.

Instead, he asked, "If you weren't a hunter, what would you be doing with your life?"

"Huh? I-I don't know."

"Well, you went to an academy. What did you get your degree in?"

"Human resource management."

His lips quirked up. "You wanted to be a *handler*?"

"Yeah? Shut up. So what."

"I'm not teasing. I think you'd be a good handler. No nonsense, keeping delinquent hunters on their toes..."

"Or maybe I'd just get a cozy office job."

"Or that."

"What was your degree in?"

"Engineering. Both mechanical and computers."

"Double-majoring computer geek? Never would have guessed." Sarcasm dripped from her tongue.

"Right. Well, my point is, I wanted to ask if, when I'm discharged, and if you're free to leave, if maybe you'd want to—and you don't have to—maybe come with me? If I just...left?"

She sat up and looked at him. Thankfully, her muted expression shifted into a small smile. "You asking me to run away with you?"

He grinned. "I might be asking that, yeah."

Her smile diminished. "Simeon wants me to train, thinks it's important, and maybe it is. Make sure I don't electrocute people by accident when I get pissed off, I guess. Find a way to control it, or suppress it. So I might need some time, here or elsewhere, if they find anyone else out there who can manipulate energy in this way. Or if not an energy elementalist, then a fire elementalist..."

"So...you might be leaving anyway."

"Yeah, maybe."

"And...would you need to be alone during this training?"

She shook her head. "Nope."

In all seriousness, Thom said, "Marry me."

Nora scoffed. "We've known each other for like a month, and for a week of that you were asleep."

"Hm, true. Marry me *someday*?"

Her lips quirked up in an unavoidable smile as she brushed her fingers through his hair. "Yeah. Okay. Someday."

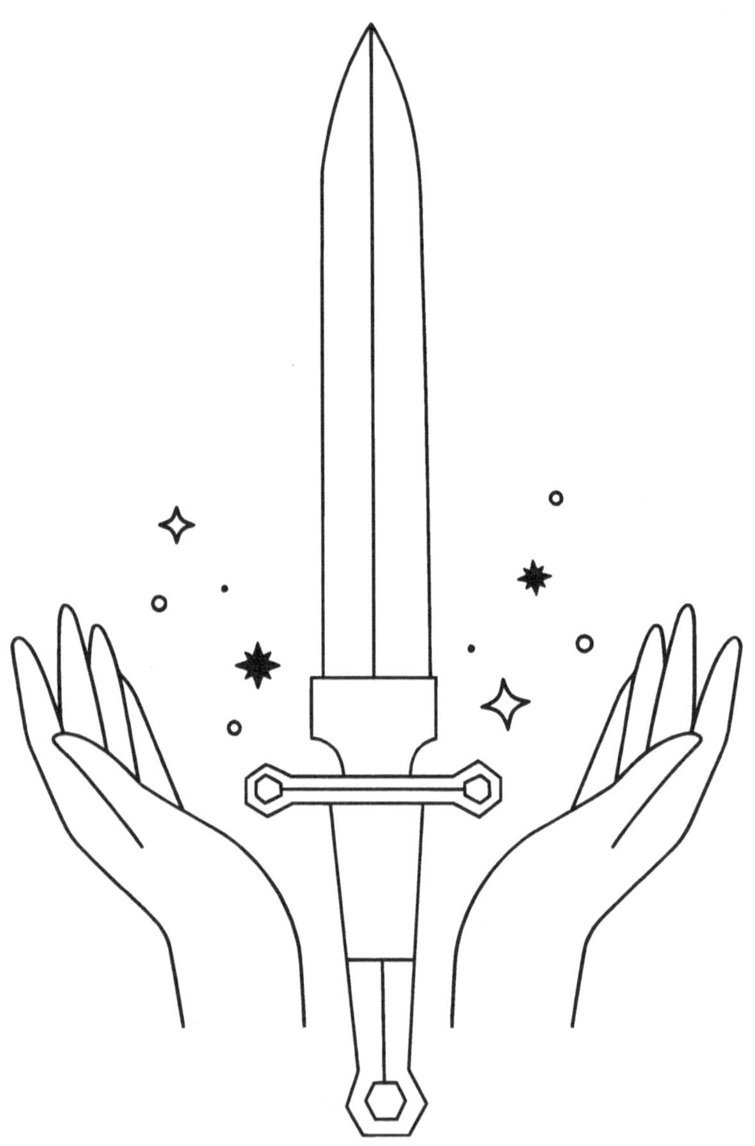

Acknowledgements

Thank you to Cinnabar Moth Publishing for being the first ever press to publish something I wrote, and thank you to the writers at Scribophile.com for critiquing the first draft of "I Just Want to Spend Christmas with My Girlfriend" which later evolved into "The Hunter & Her Girlfriend."

Thank you to all those who beta-read these stories, including Artie, Ash, Brianna, Callie, Judith, Ramey, Tilly, and in particular Jess.

Finally, thank you to those who enjoyed an unpublished story I wrote in 2012, when I was a baby writer. That story became "The Healer & The Hammer" which I hope you will enjoy just as much.

About the Author

A.M. Weald writes adult character-driven fiction in a mix of genres from the romantic to the speculative. She is a freelance editor, a semi-retired archaeologist, and a neurodivergent xennial who thinks about cats too often.

Learn more at **www.amweald.com** and sign up for her newsletter for news and updates.

Enjoyed this book? Consider leaving a review or posting about it on social media.

Other works by the author:

Even If We're Broken: a novel (2024)

Unburnt: a speculative firefighter novella (2023)